70097155

THE LOVE YOU PROMISED ME

a novel by
SILVIA MOLINA

translated by
DAVID UNGER

Curbstone Press

FIRST EDITION, 1999
Copyright © 1999 by Silvia Molina
Translation copyright ©1999 by David Unger
All Rights Reserved

Printed on acid-free paper by Best Book/Transcon Printing
Cover design: Les Kanturek

This book was published with the support of the Connecticut
Commission on the Arts, the National Endowment for the Arts,
the U.S.-Mexico Fund for Culture, and donations from many
individuals. We are very grateful for this support.

The publishers thank Barbara Rosen and Hardie St. Martin for
their help in preparing this manuscript for publication.

Library of Congress Cataloging-in-Publication Data

Molina, Silvia, 1946-
    [El amor que me juraste. English]
    The love you promised me : a novel / by Silvia Molina ;
translated by David Unger. -- 1st ed.
        p.   cm.
    ISBN 1-880684-62-4 (paper)
    I. Unger, David. II. Title.
PQ7298.23.O5A4613   1999
863--dc21   99-27587
Printed in Canada

published by
 CURBSTONE PRESS   321 Jackson Street   Willimantic, CT 06226
        phone: 860-423-5110   e-mail: info@curbstone.org
                    http://www.curbstone.org

"Then the just can also deceive?" Rachel asked.
"They can fight deception with deception," Jacob answered.
Genesis

What did you do with the love you promised me?
What have you done with the kisses I gave you?
What excuse will you give me
for not having and then destroying
the hope I had within me?

Mario de Jesús

THE LOVE YOU PROMISED ME

Chapter One

The chatter of starlings signaled the coming of night when I looked out from my balcony to the harbor. There they were, the tourists, packing the Central Plaza, the San Andrés Church, City Hall and the San Carlos, Soledad and San Francisco Hotels. They sipped beer, snacked on fish appetizers or tamales wrapped in plantain leaves under the arcades where vendors hawked, without let up, Panama hats and hand-embroidered dresses and blouses. The tourists succumbed, as I did, to the array of blue, orange, red and yellow flowers sewn into the collars and the sleeves.

And beyond San Lázaro's ramparts, I saw people starting to crowd the waterfront. I wondered what I was doing locked up inside my hotel room.

It was as if I were watching a pilgrimage: lovers walking hand in hand, boys on bikes, young girls buying ice cream or mamey and guanabana sno-cones, fathers pointing out to their children the sun about to drop below the horizon, and the Indian and mestizo women walking toward the pier to await the returning shrimp boats whose lights would turn into a floating city in front of the fortified Gulf of Mexico.

I gazed at the sky and its reflection in the sea that October evening, hoping that it was the spectacle before me that was making me feel disturbingly insignificant and helpless (or perhaps insecure or even sorry and anxious) and not the disorder and chaos in my life.

At this moment, more than at any other time, the San Lázaro sea held me in its spell because though it's normally a calm bay, the waves seemed churned by a great urgency. Hypnotized by the way the wind left its mark on the water's surface, I found myself spinning down into my memories; I drifted and went under despite my efforts to stay afloat by erasing from memory all the mistakes I had made, and pretending I could bury my actions like dropping a seed in the ground to grow a rosebush, an azalea or a hydrangea, or laying the foundation for a house or building, vainly believing I could avoid the guilt and pain that follow the careless loss of a dear pet run over right before your eyes or the sorrow you feel after burying a happy song-filled canary that gradually forgot its song as it grew old until one morning it lay stiff in a corner of its cage.

Looking out, I tried to calm myself and to somehow trick my suffering by denying it, as if you could cure pneumonia with two aspirins or an intestinal infection with a spoonful of Maalox.

The music from room 326 started again. The couple staying there—young Americans (he had blond hair, a soldier's buzz cut, and she was thin and a bit taller) who I'd seen registering earlier in the day holding a tape deck—played the same song over and over again, skipping the other cuts, as if it symbolized their relationship or was their honeymoon's theme song.

I had heard the ballad so many times that I had learned it by heart and it was driving me crazy.

> There was a boy
> a very strange and enchanted boy,
> They say he wandered very far
> very far over land and sea...

The wind kept rising, forcing me back into my room to escape the gusts whipping my hair into my eyes. A weak, almost violet sun stamped itself on the hotel's whitewashed walls. The modern rattan furniture upholstered in bright colors tried to make the room pleasant and soothing; the chairs, the vanity stool and the bedspread were festooned with orange and yellow flowers on a lime-green background and matched the curtains. In addition, the room smelled of cleanliness, brand new, like the scented wax of highly polished furniture. But I was indifferent to it, just as you can be indifferent to someone who seems repulsive and boring for having deceived you or when you realize that your interests clash like oil and vinegar or sugar and salt.

I couldn't stop myself from pacing in the room, consumed by hatred and contempt for myself. The tile floor held the damp prints of my footsteps. Coming out of the shower I had left a confusing trail on the floor, a track around the bed to the night stand and table, a crazy pattern going in and out of the bathroom, disappearing finally out the balcony door just as the music from next door seemed to get mixed up with the darkness and lose itself and unsettle me even more:

> A little shy and sad of eyes,
> but very wise was he.
> And then one day, a magic day,
> he passed my way...

I had left Eduardo's letters in a cloth-lined box on the bed: over thirty letters secured by a red ribbon, letters summarizing two stories and more importantly, one out-and-out deception, a lie, an apology, a despair of ever achieving happiness—not my happiness but Eduardo's. From a Wednesday to a Friday he built a breachless wall around himself, to protect himself from me or from my love and affection, my attachment and care, just like the San Lázaro residents had overnight destroyed a wall to give access to an avenue—city walls it had taken years to build for protection from pirates. You build slowly and carefully for someone else to wreck it in a fraction of a second.

Yet his wasn't a fragile, crumbling or easily broken wall hastily built, like the pile of letters where the black ink of

Eduardo's Mont Blanc pen linked the clever words that told lively stories filled with memories, with dreams and happiness, with life; or other letters that traced thoughts steeped in fear, sadness, desperation. It was a solid wall, not filled with declarations and pretexts because, after all, words tend to be forgotten or else you can silence, erase or cross them out. And words of love burn up and disappear simply by lighting them with the flame of hatred or lost love. I know it's difficult to battle secret habits or vices as long as they don't fill you with guilt. And the only way Eduardo could defend himself against love was by putting up a barricade that stopped him from continuing his seduction, enchantment, his charm.

I also didn't know how to combat or knock down the mental fence Eduardo had erected.

I was in San Lázaro because it seemed to be a refuge. I needed to be far off, far away from Mexico City, the accomplice that had shielded us, to try and understand what I had done with my life, to recall and exorcise my mistakes and come to a decision. I needed courage not only to accept the split, but to accept my bruised ego.

I know that running away, while helpful, was stupid. As my father once had told my brother Alberto: "No matter where you go, you'll find a roach."

He was right. Wherever I turned in San Lázaro, I saw the ruins of my life: who can escape himself?

But San Lázaro was the refuge I sought when exhaustion and grief caught up with me, because I believed that there, near the sea, the mountains and the jungle, I could cover up suffering with the discomfort of unlived memories, with the ghosts, griefs and hopes of a town and family I never knew. Because in San Lázaro everything would be new and four in the afternoon on a Monday in the fall would not be four in the afternoon on a Monday in the fall, because time in San Lázaro—like time outside the capital—moves slowly and I needed to think things over. If someone had asked me who

I was, I could give an honest answer because no one knew me there.

San Lázaro was just another stop on my way to Ithaca. No one there needed to know more than that I was a tourist, a foreigner, a traveler. I wouldn't have to explain things or reveal the truth: the double life I had dragged all the way to the sea to dump one of them there, leave it abandoned to its fate.

Besides, Eduardo wouldn't come to San Lázaro to insist, after another silent interval, on apologizing again, complaining about his wife, his work, his isolation, going over all his problems for us to end up once more arguing about guilt and futility.

I traveled to that place not only to explore the town, but because I was sure that far from home, I'd finally be able to lie in bed until very late poring over memories or else I'd be able to fall into such a deep sleep that nightmares would not reach me. I would, therefore, realize once more that life wasn't always complicated and difficult.

I also went there for a motive I can't put into words other than to say that it was a justifiable obsession: I told my husband Rafael I would spend time searching the trail of my ancestors.

That evening, watching the sun set from my balcony, I thought about my future. It was hard to put my thoughts together; I only felt dejected and bitter, a kind of hopelessness that stirred up a desire to throw myself upon the bed and sleep, not to think about anything, not even about my children. Not even to get dressed or eat something.

All the time I gave up for Eduardo seemed a dream in which there was nothing for me to grasp. I remained myself in our relationship while Eduardo fooled himself by playing a role he hadn't been prepared to play; when he had to face up to this, he lost his nerve.

My ancestors are buried somewhere in San Lázaro. They came from Spain, fell in love with the village and dropped anchor there. My father's parents lived there, as did his grandfather's grandparents, and that led me to fantasize I was connected to a land which had remained undiscovered and nonexistent to my brothers and me. The difference is that my brothers never showed the least interest in searching for our roots since they're completely tied up to the life we lived in Mexico City.

San Lázaro is an abandoned port. It's been years since vessels with large loads have come to it because a planned railroad link stayed on the drawing boards in the 1900s and there was no effective way to transport goods to the Mexican interior. From then on, nothing but Carnival, street fairs, sweet sixteen parties, baptisms, *Te Deums*, weddings and political conflicts have taken place in that small town, rendering life dull, even exasperating. There's no set trade or industry, no movies to show the latest releases (The Garden Cinema, San Lázaro's first movie house, was roofless then and still is now, showing Cantinflas and Pedro Infante films). There's only a university-affiliated theater, no concert halls, no bookstores...there's nothing but cafés, lots of them, where mostly men and once in a while women pass the afternoon playing dominoes, reading the paper, or discussing politics.

San Lázaro is a town that lives off its dreams of greatness during the colonial period. If it weren't for tourists (small in number), the shrimp shipped by air and the oil wells on the coast, San Lázaro would've had to move elsewhere or else totally disappear. Yet its colonial buildings make it unique, at the edge of a tranquil and quiet ocean which can be seen from anywhere in town.

My father hardly ever mentioned San Lázaro or his family. Whenever we broached the subject, he'd say nothing or begin talking about something else. But when we were alone with her, our mother would tell us that her in-laws were snobbish—restless, authoritarian and spiritually fickle and, like most families of Spanish origin, wealthy.

According to Miguel—a native I met during my trip, a kind of guardian angel who flung off the evil spirits besieging me and pointed me to the promised land—my ancestors owned one of the most successful lumberyards in town. Tall ships were built and vessels from Spain were repaired there. When boats stopped coming back and forth, my relatives traded logwood, chicle, sisal and sugarcane; and when the market for these items died, they squandered their fortunes and in time became bureaucrats, lawyers and doctors. And long before I felt Miguel's power of the sword opening a path beyond my fears and distrust, I wanted to reconstruct piece by piece that history, that unread past my father always silenced with more than enough reason.

I believed my parents had fled village boredom as soon as they could, to settle in Mexico City where life was always changing; they never gave a second thought to what they had left behind because it didn't add up to much. But during this trip, a cousin of my father would reveal to me, relishing the secret, the true story of our escape from San Lázaro.

I looked at the sky until it darkened and I could see the stars that the Mexico City night sky denies us. I stepped back into my room, sat down on the bed and picked up Eduardo's letters.

The envelopes were all the same color and size. They were united by the angular print, identical stamps. Dr. Carillo's letters are beautiful as objects. Exactly alike to a T: the address of the sender and receiver written at the same height. This makes me think, quite often now, that Eduardo is not just an orderly person: he's obsessed with being neat, clean, and rigorous. A man who's not been able to and never will break his rigid habits and beliefs.

Sometimes Eduardo's letters were long, full of details; at other times almost as brief as a telephone message or a telegram, painfully to the point:

Marcela, I won't see you again.

I reread them many times, thinking I might be able to figure out the end. I had splayed them out like playing cards: hearts, spades, diamonds, clubs. Or according to the message: love, quarrel, hope, desire, leaving a separate pile for those concerning separation, the ones underscoring the hopelessness of it all. I'd rearrange the contents according to my mood, omitting the controversial and unhappy parts. I couldn't keep from creating a story distinct from reality, except for that night in which I decided to read them all over again.

I lifted my eyes and looked at myself in the mirror above the vanity. I saw a person I both recognized and didn't recognize, since the she seemed so aloof, so different from the way I am normally when I find myself somewhere, even if I'm not dressed appropriately or my shoes are scuffed. My eyes gave me away: I could see my vulnerability in the circles under them. I was sorely lacking the experience to end an affair. "I'm here, alone," I thought, "because this is where I want to be, because only here will I be able to make sense of things, reorder my life, find a way out." Hearts, diamonds, clubs, spades. Love, hope, desire, struggle.

From my bed I could see that it was a cloudless night; if it weren't for the music from the room next door, I wouldn't have felt like crying.

> ...and while we spoke of many things,
> fools and kings, this he said to me:
> The greatest thing
> you'll ever learn is to love
> and be loved in return.

Fear forced me to put off reading the letters and go out once more to the balcony. The sky was full of stars, the quarter moon rising. I thought about myself. No. I didn't know then nor do I now know the meaning of resignation. Perhaps I should be looking for resistance and rebellion instead. Meekness and conformity were aspects of my mother that I hated. I had the right to live a more exciting life than the one I'd been taught to expect. If you want something and do nothing to get it, you're lost.

Chapter Two

I first met Eduardo at his office in 1994 when the country's political situation was in chaos, and violence and uncertainty were everywhere. From New Year on, we woke up each day to unlikely events: the armed conflict in Chiapas; the murder of the PRI candidate Luis Donaldo Colosio; the suspension of the power struggle among the various PRI factions; the shrewdness of Manuel Camacho Solís, rector one day, Secretary of State the next, then part of the Chiapas Peace Commission and finally hinting that he might announce his candidacy for President of Mexico; the emergence of Subcomandante Marcos, the guerrilla poet who seemed to be all over the news; the announcement of Ernesto Zedillo as Colosio's successor; the clashes over electoral reform; the television debate among the PRD, the PAN, and the PRI candidates; the selection of José Francisco Ruiz Massieu as the PRI Secretary General; José Francisco Ruiz Massieu's murder; the setting up of commissions and the naming of special prosecutors to investigate the murders of Colosio and Ruiz Massieu and the selection of a prosecuting attorney to try and uncover the truth about these assassinations; the kidnapping of Alfredo Harp Helú, a well-known banker; the disappearance of Congressman Muñoz Rocha.

Like everyone else, Rafael kept up with the latest developments, especially those events that affected his clients in Chiapas. He was so concerned and distracted that he couldn't imagine I would sink into such an intense stupor, a dark sleep, so deep a personal depression that it couldn't be put into words: like when your clothes don't fit and you don't like what you see in the mirror, but you continue to overeat instead of dieting, or keep working at a job that doesn't satisfy you and, instead of quitting, forget to deal with your own unhappiness.

How could I imagine my life could change if it was so insignificant? I had plans, desires and longings that went unfulfilled, not because I didn't know what I wanted or because of broken promises, forgetfulness or the inability to come to a decision; rather because life plays with you and makes its choices without counting on you. When things began to change, I had a husband I respected (though he paid more attention to his clients than to me), two healthy children, stubborn and unruly like all preadolescents, and a job I liked.

My previously healthy 83-year-old mother suddenly became ill. My two older brothers wouldn't take care of her, arguing that they (like my husband) worked from dawn to dusk and their wives didn't have time (nor the interest) to take care of their mother-in-law (I worked, they didn't). Moreover, they made just enough money to cover their bare necessities. My brother Alberto is an engineer and his friends say that he's the most penny-pinching contractor they know and he's made a bundle. My other brother, despite the ups-and-downs, lives like a king, better not ask how he does it. Rafael and I were not having a hard time of it either, of course: Rafael works long and hard, as I do.

These are some of the irreparable changes that occur in families. You become selfish and you want to maintain your freedom and independence at all costs. Even I skirted my responsibilities though I knew that like plants and pets, the elderly need care and, like infants, lots of love.

Not only did I have a sick mother to take care of, but a husband clothed in mystery that imbued his life with a kind of secret code—a world he kept from the rest of us, including me, an unapproachable world that, like that of my brothers, allowed his ambition and his work to come before his very own family. His job kept him away from home all day and a good part of the night. And when he finally came back, he was exhausted, full of one-word answers, too tired to make love, wanting only to sleep.

Rafael lived in his world, yes, but I don't want to imply that I was unhappy at his side. What marriage is perfect? Perhaps I wanted him to make me more a part of his world outside the home. And because I was by and large happy with Rafael, my love for Eduardo was perverse, evil, and wicked.

I was raising two young boys and working in an ad agency when I was obliged to move my ailing mother into my house. It wasn't easy for anyone. My kids loved their doting grandma until the moment she moved in; though sick, she tried to discipline them in my absence and when she wanted to nap, we wouldn't let the boys make noise. Our diets also had to change; my boys hated the salt-free meals, the abundance of vegetables and fish and poultry, the lack of snacks.

I have to admit, though, that Rafael was very supportive. "Don't get rid of her bedroom; she needs to continue sleeping in her own bed, seeing her old furniture. I'll have Pancho convert Rafael and Felipe's playroom into her bedroom. We have to make a comfortable place for her."

And Pancho made sure that her furnishings and things were moved in, including a suitcase that was stored under her bed and which I didn't open until long after her death. I had no idea it was there, that she had had it put away or, more likely, hidden it there.

That's Rafael: always getting someone to do things. He doesn't change a light bulb, put in a nail. He's learned to give orders and that's what he does.

With mother at home, Rafael and I lost the scarce privacy we had been used to. Worse, my mother competed with him, made demands on my time and presence. I must admit that as sick as she looked, under those circumstances,

SILVIA MOLINA

she won out. It wasn't easy, but there was no other choice for me, for Rafael, or even for our boys.

My mother had sold her house much earlier and purchased a small apartment—all she needed—in the San Rafael neighborhood. She lived there with a live-in woman from Tabasco who cooked her meals, did the cleaning, gave her her medicine. At first, I would drive across Mexico City, irritated by all the traffic (I tried several routes), swallowing the smog (I'd come home with a headache and bleary eyes), having lost patience with my mother who wouldn't eat or take her medicine when I wasn't around. Finally I gave up and decided to "adopt" my mother, but her companion wouldn't come along and help me. At first I was scared, but thinking it over, it was all for the best. Mother was *my* mother, *my* patient, *my* responsibility. This was also another difficult situation because I learned to do what I had to as I went along; I hadn't been prepared in advance and here mistakes weren't allowed. I had to give her shots, take her blood pressure, every six hours give her her medicine, prepare all kinds of purees so that she would eat something...

Eduardo was the celebrity specialist and everyone said he was a great doctor. He had written a few medical books, and he was well on his way to becoming the favorite surgeon for the rich, the famous, the politically connected, the intellectuals, the millionaires. He had been recommended to Rafael because Dr. Teodoro Cesarman, The Cardiologist, my mother-in-law's doctor, was not in Mexico at the moment.

I called Eduardo and then took my mother to the hospital emergency room; among my mother's many ailments, that morning she was feeling a lot of pain in her chest. The diagnosis was angina, not a heart attack, and that's why she had to stay in the hospital where Eduardo had his office. It wasn't like that of her regular doctor, with his ultrasound and x-ray machines—Eduardo's waiting

13

room was more like an art gallery or a very tastefully furnished studio. His office had little in common with the traditional doctor's office.

During the days she was confined to the hospital, "Dr. Carrillo" was the first and last person to visit her. He would arrive in his white gown, his stethoscope dangling from his neck. After examining her, he would take off his eyeglasses, his eyes clearly tired, and sit down next to me on the sofa-bed, remaining there as if he were a family friend, as if we were in a living room at home waiting for a cup of coffee or tea. As if he were not in a rush, had nothing to do.

Sometimes he'd run into Rafael, but Rafael would run off at once, saying he had an appointment, a meeting, something to discuss with the Board of Examiners—the usual. And I suppose that Eduardo was pleased not to have to act chummy with him. Not dealing with him somehow lessened the betrayal. Looking back at it now, it was something low, vile.

Eduardo would secretly look me over, glancing discreetly at my breasts and my thighs; he'd question my convalescing mother as if he were a novelist, not a cardiologist. Dr. Carrillo had learned that Dolores Sierra de Souza was from Tabasco and had lived through the socialist and antireligious regime of Tomás Garrido Canabal.

"Doña Dolores, tell me about it," he asked softly one night.

"I don't remember anymore."

"You don't want to tell me about it?"

"It happened so long ago."

"Tell me about Garrido. Have you discussed him with Marcela?"

She had told me nothing about her time in Tabasco. Strange as it may seem, the youth of my parents remained a secret to us. We didn't even have any pictures from that era.

My mother looked at us, beginning to puff up: "They called him *El Charro Negro*. Can you imagine? A Mexican cowboy in Tabasco, in that heat, deep in the tropics? It was absurd. We all wore linen or cotton or white burlap cloth blouses. That's how the respectable people or the dignified Indians dressed. They also called him the *Macaw* because of his red and black airplane. They made fun of him because—like a parrot—he didn't know what he was talking about when he spoke."

"But what was he really like?"

"He was like a movie star—the young girls fluttered about him."

"You, too?" he teased.

"No way! I was just a kid."

"When was this?"

"Doctor, he ruled for many years. He was the provisional leader starting in 1920; then in '22 he become governor with the support of General Obregón; after the pro-Huerta revolt, he took power once more, and I think he was reelected governor in 1930. Then, luckily, he was kicked out of the country; sadly this was after he had destroyed Tabasco. Whole families had left because it was impossible to live there with him in power."

"Where did your family go?"

"To San Lázaro, where one of our uncles worked on a sisal farm."

"What was your life like then?"

While she spoke, my mother gazed unblinkingly at Eduardo; her expression was sad, almost as tired as her voice.

"My mother kept us locked in because there were so many demonstrations. It was a mess. Anticlerical and pro-prohibition protests. 'Why does he do this? Weren't his parents Christians?' my mother would ask, because Garrido wasn't satisfied with just banishing the priests from Tabasco, he wanted to throw them all out of the country. So Calles and Cárdenas went along, supporting him, while that idiot destroyed the San Rafael Church and La Conchita Cathedral.

The churches he left standing he converted into rationalist schools."

"Did you go to a rationalist school?" he asked, looking at me impishly. This bothered me.

"There were no alternatives."

"What were they like?"

"Poor, doctor. Life was hard in those days."

"I mean the rationalist schools?"

"In the open air, like farmyards."

"And what were you taught?"

"Agriculture and animal husbandry. Garrido wanted all of us to work in the fields."

"Your family was Catholic?"

"Like almost all the other families, doctor. But there was no worship, no services. Anyone caught practicing rites or protecting a priest was thrown in jail."

"Were any of your relatives imprisoned?'

My mother acted as if she were scanning her memory and Eduardo jumped ahead. "Do you remember the *Red Shirts*?"

"Of course. Daughters denounced members of their own family. They wore black skirts and red blouses. The boys wore purple shirts and black trousers and they'd ride into the churches on horseback and burn the wooden saints, steal what they could, wreck everything."

"I thought you couldn't remember, Doña Dolores?" laughed Eduardo, glancing at me.

My mother breathed deeply and added: "I want to go to my own house now, doctor." She then corrected herself. "To my daughter's house."

And I realized that it wasn't easy for her to live with us, either.

"Soon now, ma'am. As soon as you've gotten back your schoolgirl's heart."

"That won't be easy," she countered.

16

"Not so hard. See, you said you remembered nothing about Garrido. You'll have to help us."

She suddenly grew animated. "Let me tell you what we had to repeat in school."

And she recited it as if she were giving us a kitchen recipe:

> With no liquor and no priests,
> Tabasco grows full of pride.
> Working hard in the fields
> producing tomorrow's riches.
>
> So long corrupt old clerics,
> sellers of indulgences.
> Here in Tabasco, Garrido
> has awakened our consciences.

When Eduardo left later that night, I had my mother repeat those verses; I jotted them down in my notebook to read to Rafael later.

"Did you know that an Englishman wrote a novel about Tabasco under Garrido's rule?" Eduardo asked her.

"No."

"It's a grim novel, ma'am."

"Then he's told the truth."

"How old were you when you left Tabasco?"

"Maybe 15 or 16. We went away because we were the last of our family there. They had all gone elsewhere in search of freedom and work."

I truly enjoyed Eduardo's company and conversation, and I began to put my makeup on carefully before he came. In other words, to spin my net while he flaunted his feathers, showed the reach of his charm. I put on my makeup meticulously, there was nothing mechanical about it: it was as if I were creating a work of art no longer meant for Rafael. I went in for dresses that masked my thinness, I brushed my hair with great care...I'd do all the things that men and women do to seduce and capture the opposite sex.

When Eduardo discharged my mother from the hospital, we went to his office every week or two; the paintings on his office walls reminded me very much of Dr. Cesarman's office. There were canvases by painters whose names I didn't recognize, but there were also paintings by María Izquierdo, Juan Soriano and Francisco Toledo. If my mother-in-law's doctor had been in Mexico, I would never have met Eduardo.

"Aren't you afraid someone will steal them?" I asked him one day. He told me they were not insured but were a part of his life and work—to remove them would be criminal, like not having music at your wedding when you can well afford it or serving a house wine at a baptism when your cellar's full of good wine.

Behind his desk he had a small, but gorgeous, Tamayo that his patients were obliged to admire. It was his favorite, so he said.

My mother endured angina and the threat of a heart attack, the next logical development. According to the tests and examinations Eduardo ordered for her, we found out that her condition had developed from high blood loss caused by colon cancer. Despite the frequent blood transfusions, my mother got sicker and became bedridden. Eduardo then started paying house calls. Even if we hadn't phoned him, he'd stop by unexpectedly to visit out of courtesy and friendship.

One night I walked with him as far as the street and asked the inevitable question: "She doesn't have long to live, does she, doctor?"

He didn't answer. Eduardo opened the car door, hesitated for a few seconds and turned toward me. "I shouldn't say it, but I've fallen in love with you, Marcela."

I didn't say a word. Instead, I looked at him, taken aback, and focused—one of those absurd moments life offers us—

18

on his gray wool suit and blue tie with the fine yellow stripes. My heart was pounding, but I went back into the house as if nothing had happened to read the Bible to my mother who was waiting for me, as she did every night. I think she had begun reading it as a young girl; she was like a Seventh Day Adventist since it was something she always had done as far back as I can remember and which she didn't force us to do. It was the source of her happiness and her peace of mind, and I really didn't mind the chore since the Old Testament stories are quite entertaining ("And Sarah, Abraham's wife, bore him no children: and she had a handmaid, an Egyptian, whose name was Hagar...") The gospels of St. Mark and St. Luke were her favorites: "Martha, Martha, thou art careful and troubled about many things: but one thing is needful."

Eduardo is a thin man, of average height, with a friendly and guileless face, twenty years older than me. Gray hair, a sharp gaze and stooped shoulders contribute to giving him a respectable air. He carries himself well, has an even temperament and, like all seducers, is a married man.

During Eduardo's subsequent visits, I struggled against myself and tried to avoid his eyes. He'd examine my mother, stay for the coffee or whiskey I offered him because I'm contrary and because I truly wanted to delay his leaving; he'd joke with my mother, raise her spirits a bit and search my eyes for some kind of sign which I denied him. A battle raged inside me between my mother's illness and Eduardo's seductiveness, between my fondness for Rafael and my interest in Eduardo. I allowed that struggle to triumph over me rather than put an end to it or make a choice.

The morning arrived when we hospitalized my mother for a colon operation. When they opened her up, they saw how far the cancer had spread. Eduardo suggested that I bring her back home and wait for the end. She shouldn't have to die in the discomfort and austerity of a hospital. As Rafael had once said, it was important for her to die in her own bed, with her daughter and grandchildren at her side.

Her final suffering didn't last long, but my failing mother would lie there as if she were on a bed of thorns, hardly moving, not opening her eyes. She moaned even while asleep under the effect of sedatives.

The cancer had also spread to her brain and her bone marrow. I stopped brushing her hair to avoid irritating the tumor protruding from her cranium and forehead—it now affected her speech and made her call me *Cemarla*. My son Felipe was the one who realized she was saying my name. It was difficult figuring out what else she said. Felipe, in particular, would come into her room at all hours and sit down at her bedside, not say a word, not knowing what to say. Rafael, the eldest, however, hardly spent any time with her.

Whenever we'd go out for a snack or were alone, he'd say to me with fear in his voice: "I don't want grandma to die."

And I didn't know how to prepare him for it. How can you prepare a child to face the death of his loved ones? I couldn't find a better way than to have them live their own normal lives; not even at the end did I try to stop their yelling and fighting, prevent them from inviting friends over to the house for dinner or to do homework. I did nothing to stop their horsing around, the messes they made, their tantrums.

Rafael insisted that I hire a nurse, but I didn't want to. I sensed that my mother would die just at the moment I left her side, and I knew I'd never forgive myself for it. I thought my mother was once again just a child who, more than simple care, needed affection—to hear a recognizable voice to assure her that she wouldn't die like a pauper.

Sitting there beside her at night, I would remember the times I hated or loved her as a child, when my mother was the center of the universe, when that thinning white hair she washed with so much care had been black, thick and shiny. I remembered when she bought my first school uniform in La Ciudad de México shop downtown, on one side of the *Zócalo*; to get there we took the city bus down streets lined with colonial buildings and churches I had never seen before. I remember choosing the outfit with the kind of excitement usually reserved for a birthday party dress.

I remembered the time my mother scolded me when I vomited over and over: "If you throw up once more, Marcela, I'm going to spank you."

Back then I hadn't understood that she was frightened to death, terrified as I would later be during those endless days and nights when I wanted to scream: "If you complain once more, Mom, I'm going to spank you."

Very often I would recall my mother's face on the afternoon they told us that Dad had had a heart attack at the office. At the time she had said things to me like "Get away from here. Leave me alone. Go study," or "Stop bothering me." And I acted as if I didn't know her, and swallowed my anger because I was suffering as much as she but had no one to comfort me. I saw her in my memory with the same paleness and the same sickly eyes with which she had left the hospital. But my mother had recovered from her husband's death as I would undoubtedly recover from the death hovering in that room I rarely left—I had requested a complete leave of absence from work to take care of my mother.

What other images came back?

My mother wearing a checkered apron in the kitchen preparing Tabasco appetizers—bean tamales for my brothers or breaded pampano for me. Mother in her rocker knitting vests and scarves for my father, following her soap opera on the radio or sitting by the record player, listening to the records my father would put on. Mother leading me by the hand along Mazatlán Avenue where we picked up the dates that dropped from the date palms on the promenade. My mother, slender and dignified as never before, dressed in navy blue satin for my wedding; my mother bathing my own children for the very first time...I also remembered the day I had my first period and she put a pair of old gold earrings on my ears and said, "My mother gave me these when the same thing happened to me," instead of explaining to me what was happening.

My mother was a humble, calm woman. Someone who never asked for more than my father could provide. Someone who never imagined life could be different although that wasn't why she didn't know how to face life when it presented itself with all the coarseness and cruelty of the unexpected. She always gave us what she could from her spending money without going against our father's wishes since his orders were for her more than commandments (I don't know what she thought after she found out the truth). And she'd stretch her pocket money to pay for our studies. Later, when I got rid of her old clothes, I realized that her dresses had aged as she had aged, that rarely did she allow herself to dress stylishly.

Since I went through my mother's death without Rafael's company and with my brothers away, Eduardo became my partner, the only one with whom I shared my wordless despair.

One night I found my mother crying silently and grew frightened. Her eyes had sunk, her face was ashen and more deeply creased, bathed in sweat, as I had never seen her before. She was struggling, not against suffering, but against her own end. I knew that death hovered in the room and, as with everything that we know nothing about, I was terrified.

I had never felt the mystery of death—that, is, the exact moment in which a person stops being what he was, when he no longer *is* and becomes *something* that has no place, no place to be put, can't be protected or stored. My father had died in his office (that's what we were told); and I never found out why (perhaps because the firm didn't want it known that he had died there or had died somewhere where he shouldn't have been), but they brought him home in a car, sitting up between two of his colleagues, his hat on his head and around his neck (perhaps to hold it up) a blue scarf my mother had just finished knitting. They carried him out of the car in a chair, as if he were ailing (I suppose so the neighbors wouldn't think he was dead) and once inside the house, they laid him on the bed so mother could dress him in his very best suit. And so I saw my father sleeping; that's the image of his death that stayed with me, not the moment when life flees and those who survive burst into tears or are unable to say a word.

My father's death was doubly painful. Two of his other children, younger than me, came to the wake as if they had been formed from thin air. It was completely unexpected and shocking, something my mother had no knowledge of or hadn't told us about and which she accepted in silence while my brothers and I burned in shame and grief and disbelief. Well, I didn't see my father die; his death was presented to us as something already done and I accepted it as such or, perhaps, with rage and the sense of not having had the time to argue about it with him or to make up. But my mother's death threatened to ambush me in the night like a snake about to spring and strangle me without warning.

That mystery, of a rupture which is one kind of death, can also be felt in love relationships. Someone like Eduardo all of a sudden tells you that he doesn't love you anymore (done deal) and your affection has no rhyme or reason to be and there's no place to put it or justify it. It's of no use. You don't know what to do with it, it no longer *is* except as *something* pointless which you must get rid of immediately. However, when a relationship gradually disintegrates and it only waits for the right moment to pounce and wound you, you feel a constant panic. The difference is that you know the blow is coming even if you don't know when or how.

I was sitting in an armchair next to my mother, drying her sweat with Kleenex. "She's going away," I thought dumbfounded. "She's leaving. This time she's really leaving."

"Oh, God, help her. She was a good woman!" I prayed, taking her hand and forgetting, once and for all, the quarrels we had had.

Like everyone else, she had weaknesses that I hated, like the way she overprotected my brothers and was terrified of my father.

I felt her icy fingers; I stroked them, trying to give her courage. I wanted her to cry out in pain, turn over her food tray, but the tears that leaked from my mother's eyes made me feel heartless, cruelly impotent. "God, help her, please help her!" I kept pleading over and over in my head.

"I'm here with you. Do you hear? I'm with you, Mommy. I was recalling how happy we were when we lived in the Condesa neighborhood and you'd take me to pick up the dates that fell from the palm trees, remember?"

My mother didn't open her eyes, never answered as if she hadn't heard. So I went on talking and talking to keep her from leaving, to snatch her away from death. I spoke to her and stroked her hands between mine.

"Do you remember the first time you took us to Cuernavaca on vacation? Do you remember that little hotel right in the center of town? When I woke up the following morning I was frightened by the wooden ceiling rafters. I didn't recognize the room and was afraid to look around. 'Where am I?' I asked myself. 'Where?' I tried real hard to remember how I had gotten there. Mommy, a dog suddenly started howling and I thought: 'There are no dogs in my house, I never hear barking from anywhere nearby.' Mom, it was your voice, your sweet and soft, perhaps happy and cheery, voice that calmed me down. You were talking to Daddy. I'll never forget it. You said to him: 'Why don't we go have breakfast near the park, in one of those restaurants with a terrace where you can see the jacarandas blossoming on the boulevard? I'll wake up the kids.' Your voice, mommy, just your voice drove off my fears and made me remember we were on holiday. That's why I'm talking to you. I want you to hear me. I want you to know that I'm here, you've had a bad dream. It'll soon be over and you'll be okay, you'll see, dear Mommy."

My mother kept sweating. I was about to call Eduardo to see if he could give her something to keep her from dying, but I just gave up. I realized she was tired of it and wanted only to die. I thought: "What right do I have to make her departure more difficult?"

Finally, just around dawn, she had a moment of lucidity and wanted to tell me something, but she mixed up her syllables. I was so tired or nervous or scared that I didn't understand what she was saying till much later.

"*Cemarla*," she whispered. "*Now going.*"

"What is it, Mommy?"

She breathed harshly and then easily, without effort, till her head fell to one side.

"She's gone," I told Rafael, waking him up. "Please call my brothers and Dr. Carrillo. I suppose someone needs to write up the death certificate."

"Why didn't you wake me?"

"I had no time."

"Are you okay?"

I felt alone, terribly alone, with no desire to cry, nothing more.

Eduardo gave me a hug I didn't want to pull away from. Both of us had held back so much, but the resistance had finally dissolved. I gave in to it and started crying. With his gentle arms Eduardo held my body and I yielded to his embrace.

I was just getting over my mother's death when one morning the phone rang in my small office at the advertising agency.

"I've been thinking of you, Marcela. How are you?"

"Fine, Eduardo. And you?"

"I'm in love."

Dr. Carrillo's magical spell made me see a different future. I had put off enjoying myself, showing my feelings openly, harboring any hope. I wanted to act irresponsibly and I did. I wanted to reorder my present life which was smothering me, and I did. I wished to invent a story with its own rules, and I did. I longed to play a different role than I was used to playing, and I did. I invested the energy that I had previously given to Rafael and my children, and which had almost vanished into sheer exhaustion and fear during my mother's agony, into the sudden appearance of Dr. Carrillo.

Tempted by the demon of madness and boredom, by curiosity, by the perverse and adventurous spirit of my ancestors, I wrote Eduardo a letter one afternoon and opened up a new post office box.

I want to know, Eduardo, how a doctor, an intellectual like yourself, falls in love. I want to find out how a man sees himself or reinvents himself; how a man like you, Eduardo, falls in or out of love. I don't want to see you: I know that if you allow yourself to be carried away with your emotions and instincts, you will always be unhappy.

Write to me, Eduardo, tell me the story of your life.

Chapter Three

After ordering a salad and a coffee up to my room, I went down the hall to fill the ice bucket that was on my bureau; then I took out a small bottle of whiskey from the minibar. I lit a Marlboro, while I weighed whether or not to read Eduardo's letters at the table near the window. I wanted both to read and not read his letters. I hesitated because I wished to protect my feeling of safety, the attitude that I knew what I was doing.

I looked up and toward the waterfront. People were still walking about. Young men parked their cars or sat on benches drinking while girls walked together in small groups, perhaps waiting for the moment when the young men would join them and walk by their sides. They'd strike up a conversation and end up either at the Hotel Fénix disco or sitting under the arcade of the main square or simply walking back and forth along the waterfront. The palm fronds along the avenue bowed humbly before the wind but the people, instead of being annoyed by the sea gusts, seemed to revel in them.

My heart raced as I undid the red bow and opened one of the letters. My hands, which resemble my father's—pale and slender, with elongated fingers and rounded short nails—, began to tremble as his had during the last months of his life.

The envelopes seemed even whiter under the lamplight. I drank half the whiskey, and my heart started pounding impatiently as I read:

Marcela, the color of the envelope, the size of your script, drew my attention. I immediately removed it from my pile of mail and took it with me to my office. When I put on my glasses and read your name, my heart raced either out of impatience or happiness, like when you wake up from a happy dream and all at once realize you can't remember it.

"Good morning, doctor," my nurse said to me.

"Good morning, Matilde," I replied, handing her some x-rays to be filed away.

"Do you want your phone messages, doctor?"

"Not now. And don't forward any phone calls either." I wanted to be alone and quiet with you.

Once in my office, I tossed my jacket on the armchair and, while loosening my tie, glanced around the room; my eyes settled happily on the Julio Castellanos painting that my wife had purchased at auction. I don't know if you remember it, Marcela, but it depicts a young woman lost in thought, a sad air enveloping her. Its gentle feeling reminds me of you each time I look at the painting. I imagine you are here with me.

I didn't know why you were writing to me, Marcela. I couldn't stop remembering you sitting there, facing me, smiling nervously: the way you would get lost worrying over your mother's illness. Your restless eyes troubled me. Don't think that we doctors are merely robots who attend to patients and their families.

I thought it was a short note thanking me for caring for your mother which, believe me, had an ulterior motive, given my affection for you.

It's not so rare to receive, with the other mail that sometimes gets forwarded to me by the journal editors, the kind of note or a letter from someone who wants to share his response to my research or articles I publish; I save a few, out of respect for the individuals who took the time to write to me, but I've never allowed myself to be influenced by the flattery though I have, on occasion, been affected by the critics. But your letter,

Marcela took me by surprise and filled me with hope. Believe me, at my age, dreams make you younger.

You propose that we write to one another...Right? To have me answer your questions, just because...you are—how should I put it?—interested in the human side of a doctor, of an "intellectual like you." You want to find out, you emphasize, how a man sees or invents himself, how a man like me falls either in or out of love. A man—you insist—like you, Eduardo." I'm not altogether sure of the rules of the game, Marcela, when you know that if you were to pick up the phone and call me, I would come running. Emotions and impulsive behavior don't always lead to unhappiness.

That you don't want to see me, while I'm dying to see you, is a strange challenge for a man my age and for people in our situation. You've stirred in me, an elderly man, the desire to do something crazy.

How does a man like me fall in or out of love, Marcela? Tell me, write to me how a woman like you falls in or out of love and we'll be on the same playing field, don't you think?

How has Eduardo Carrillo fallen in love? Do you really want to know? Right now I'm recalling José Emilio Pacheco's novel Battles in the Desert. *Have you read it? Like Carlos, the book's main character, I first fell in love with my second grade teacher when I was a boy. Though you might not believe it, I dreamed that I would crawl into her bed and wake up nice and warm snuggling beside her. Then I fell in love with Micaela, a young girl from my home town...But my first serious romance occurred when I was just beginning my medical studies in the old Palace of the Inquisition facing Santo Domingo Plaza downtown.*

I had rented an apartment in a building on Cumbres de Maltrata in the Narvarte district. There I lived with some other guys like myself who came from the provinces and had little money. One of them, Raúl Gutiérrez Bueno, who is now one of Mexico's leading internists, asked if he could borrow my record player for a party I had no intention of attending.

"*Damn, Raúl, Monday we have a major test in anatomy,*"
I said.

Truth was I was reading Tropic of Capricorn:

> For there is only one great adventure and that is
> inward, toward the self; and for that, time nor space
> nor even deeds matter.

*I memorized those words I had underlined in the novel
because,, ever since, I have suspected that the only true journey
is toward the self, because I was looking for a way out that
would reconcile me to the emptiness that took away my sleep.
Did I really want to be a doctor? Memorize all the p's and q's
of the Quiroz text?*

> *Bregma*: junction of the coronal and sagittal sutures.
> *Glabella*: highest point on the supraorbital ridges.
> *Gnathion*: most inferior point of the mandible in
> the midline.

*See, I can still recite from the manual as if I were studying
it now.*

*Would I have to put up with Doctor Nava's irony for the
rest of the year, his ridicule and games, inhaling formaldehyde
and other putrid odors in the dissection lab? Is that what I
wanted, to cut open corpses donated by the morgues? Is that
why I had given up San Bernardino, the inheritance from my
grandfather? Those were my thoughts: "Only one great
adventure...," when Raúl came into my room.*

"*Lalo, the records aren't dropping. Come and join us for a
drink. Don't be that way. Come on!*"

*It was an old record player my grandmother had given me
for my 17th birthday so I could listen to what was then my
favorite music—back then, you see, I had just discovered jazz.
I took care of those records as if you couldn't find others in all
of Mexico City which had everything—in sharp contrast to*

my village. Duke Ellington's "Sophisticated Lady," Peggy Lee's "Why Don't You Do Right," Dexter Gordon's "For All We Know," Charlie Parker's "Round Midnight"...music not popular in your times, Marcela, records that obviously I had not loaned for the party.

I put on a shirt simply to go out of my room and tell Raúl what to do: "You've got to jiggle the arm so the records drop."

Just then a young gypsy-like girl came up to me.

"What are you doing?" she asked.

"Losing out because I didn't know you were coming to this party," I replied teasingly, because I liked her eyes and her Spanish accent.

It was Carmen. She was pretty, the first girl I'd ever met with such self-confidence. "So what are you waiting for? Let's dance," and she dragged me with her.

And when much later Carmen came with me into my room to get the records we were to listen to at that time of night, she closed the door. She was the one who unbuttoned my shirt and transported me to a place I had never been before. Many months later I would think of that place as a maze whose way out had been so hard to find because it wasn't the way toward love but the way toward wickedness and jealousy.

How does a man fall in love, you ask. I don't know if you'd really be pleased to know about the adventure that followed, the miserable journey into my innermost being.

I shared that first passion with Carmen all the way. We spent the entire night talking about peaceful Mexico City—it was another era—, her Spanish family, her businessman father, her soon-to-be wedding to an actor who was on tour and to whom she was already engaged—she wore a small diamond ring on her left hand.

When I dropped her off at home, in her own car, her mother asked me as she opened the door if I knew that Carmen was engaged. I said yes though my head was spinning and I knew how free Carmen had been in my bed and the games we'd played in the car...

Marcela, for five months I lived in hell with that woman. I even worried about myself, but I fended off guilt. I believed I would capture life with her when, in fact, life was escaping from me. I actually wanted to see her destroyed, brought down in the same way that she had demolished me, forcing me to despise myself.

Not until that moment had I noticed the meaning of those last few lines. "I wanted to see her destroyed, brought down in the same way that she had demolished me, forcing me to despise myself." Hadn't the same thing happened to me? Hadn't Eduardo demolished me? Hadn't he forced me to despise myself? I'm not sure I wasn't starting to hate him.

Someone knocked at the door. The waiter put the tray on the bureau. I then poured myself another whiskey. Before sitting back down again, I looked through the window toward the main square. The restaurants were beginning to fill up and the people milled around the candy and refreshment stand as if it were broad daylight. Several trios, guitars in hand, offered to sing for the tourists who were dining in the open air under the arcades of those old mansions. From above, the grid of colonial streets resembled a perfect checkered pattern under the street lamps. How elegant and how mysterious was this city to me. I could have spent the whole night gazing down at it.

I went back to the table and to the letter:

How does a man fall in love, Marcela? I could say that it's like going to war, when love appears in savage form. I can say that I've fallen in love often like a loyal soldier, because love has never come to me gently. But is this what you want to know? Or do you want to know how I fell in love with you?

Let me tell you something: I liked the way your letter began. I suffered a kind of pleasant jolt. That's how one learns to bear passion, with a sudden impulse to taste joy or grief.

I read it admiring the small and round letters, fantasizing that I could discover the woman hiding behind each word.

When do you want to see me, Marcela? What you propose is a different game, but it might end up being a unique experience if we know how to enjoy it.

How does a woman fall in love, Marcela? How have you fallen in love?

Eduardo Carrillo

All of Eduardo's letters were signed, as if he had nothing to fear from our exchange.

I picked up my glass and walked around the room tinkling the ice cubes. A suffocating heat, a raging heat, coursed through my body. I never sent Eduardo the letter where I told him what it was like living by his side. I wrote it like a homework assignment whose grade would determine if I could take the next level course. When I was about to give it to him, it was too late: I had flunked. So I made corrections.

I looked for it among the letters from Doctor Carrillo. It had to be there, and I hoped I hadn't lost it or ripped it up in a pointless fit of fury.

Opening it I saw Eduardo's face: the lines on his forehead and at the edge of his nose and mouth that defined his stubborn character and the experience that life had given him. But he had, as I almost always remember him, a peaceful smile and eyes that revealed tenderness. Doctor Carrillo could be so delicate...Behind his efficient exterior, there was a warm and playful person full of tenderness.

Suddenly I was seized by such deep regret that I wanted to knock on the room next door and tell the couple listening to the tune that began "There was a boy..." as if it were the only song, to stop the tape deck, once and for all, or let me in. Instead, I read my letter out loud, slightly embarrassed, as if trying to block out the music:

Eduardo, I never told you how women fall in love. I guess because I've never been sure. Now I know that we fall in love on impulse like Eve, with total abandon like Sarah, Abraham's wife. Didn't she pretend she was his sister when the pharaoh insisted she join his harem and didn't Sarah give her servant Hagar unto Abraham so that she could bear the son that her own sterility denied her?

We fall in love, Eduardo, with the lust of Lot's wife, with the delicacy and the certainty of Rebekah, the one who drew water for Abraham's camels and without thinking said "I will go."

We fall in love with Rachel's rapture, she who competed with her sister Leah for the love of Jacob; and with Leah's patience who was rejected by Jacob and still prayed to God.

We fall in love with the trickery of Tamar, she who disguised herself as a whore to seduce Judah; with the fascination of Dinah, she who was defiled by Shechem, provoking the wrath of his brothers; with the lustfulness of Bathsheba who seduced David.

We fall in love with the tenacity of Ruth, the Moabite; with the passion of Rabbah, the streetwalker of Jericho; with the shamelessness of Zuleika, the one who went after Joseph with words, gifts and love potions.

We fall in love with the dishonor of Dinah, with Drusilla's licentiousness, with the lies of Sapphira, with the resignation of Mary Magdalene, with the faith of Elizabeth, mother of John the Baptist, with the betrayal of Delilah, with the power of Deborah, and with the sweetness of the Shulamite.

We fall in love with the innocence of the four thousand virgins that were bequeathed to Benjamin's sons, with the bitterness of Mara, with Martha's luck, with the servility of Rhoda, the infidelity of Gomer, Hosea's concubine.

That's how I have fallen in love, Eduardo, with my heart, my stomach and my guts; with courage and fear and tenacity. Falling in love does not mean finding joy. I say this now perhaps because I am filled with rage, a silent rage that puts our past in balance. I weep not out of regret, Eduardo, but because I cannot have you, because I know myself too well to know that I don't desire you without modesty and regret. My passion rises above the grief that I am experiencing.

We always have to choose, I know. And there are times when we give up happiness though later we think that it was happiness which left us while we dawdled and preferred to feel each minute of our existence intensely.

Peace can abandon us, Eduardo, the stability of marriage disappear, even the death of our loved ones can lock us in. Love can be deceitful and that's why we give in to the pleasures that hold off the emptiness. I chose you in cold blood and I got lost in the ecstasy. I surrendered myself, Eduardo; and you deceived me and were afraid to try happiness.

Maybe Eduardo was right: loving him did not give me any rights, not even the right to claim the promises made, those not kept in mind.

Chapter Four

The San Andrés bells tolled, calling people to Mass, just as the harbor was coming out of its slumber. I woke up, not remembering when I had fallen asleep. Putting on the light, I looked at the table: Eduardo Carrillo's letters were strewn around on it, but I couldn't remember if I had read them. This fact bothered me. Forgetfulness is an unmistakable omen, an indication of exhaustion, clear-cut proof that my love was dying. I then turned my eyes toward the bureau where the waiter had left the dinner tray. The food hadn't been touched, but I didn't feel hungry, just a deep thirst as if I'd eaten too much popcorn at the movies or finished off all the little whiskey bottles in the minibar. I had no idea when I had fallen asleep, though I did remember finally seeing the harbor empty and the main square clear of people.

The bells continued tolling, calling parishioners not to prayer or a funeral, but to Mass. The town awakening occupied my thoughts, and I let it, so I wouldn't have to think about Eduardo or Rafael—I'd forgotten to call him the night before—or about my children or anything that would bewilder me because I was enjoying the calming effect of the clanging of the bells.

It was a drawn-out, joyful sound. I recalled a few verses by López Velarde, my father's favorite poet—"And the crazy laughing bronze of that defiant bell"—and cheered up. I also recalled my father reciting:

> Girlfriend walking away
> perhaps I will never see you again...

It hadn't been a bad choice, after all, to come to San Lázaro to reassess my life.

The town mothers, dressed in thin light-colored clothes, would just be finishing serving breakfast or arriving at work or at the school where they taught, or were just walking out of their house on the way to the Mass announced by the bells; and the Indian women, in their native outfits embroidered with bright flowers, would be covering their heads with their rebozos as they entered the church grounds. The night's coolness could still be felt.

The men would either be in the fields or the jungles or on the open sea or getting dressed to have breakfast with friends at a café to continue last night's conversation, to discuss women some more or to carry on the same political gossip, talk about newspaper articles or television clips. Or they'd be returning from the market or the docks wearing white guayaberas or heading off to the office.

I wasn't going to Mass and had nothing to do until nine when the Archbishop's Archives opened. I'd try to find certificates of baptism, marriage, and death for my relatives. I'd do this either out of curiosity or interest, though also as a way to pass the time in this city where there wasn't much to do and in which I didn't have a single friend.

I'd also go for lunch at the house of my father's cousin. I hadn't known he existed nor had I heard anyone talk about him and had no idea if he was still alive, but I had looked through the telephone directory and found many Souzas. I had called him, on the spur of the moment, told him who I was and he said he was a cousin of "Leandro, for God's sake, what a surprise," and I told him why I wanted to see him.

He promised me photos, in which I imagined I'd recognize myself or my brothers, whom I'd never seen again after my mother's death. They had vanished into thin air, disappeared, been erased from the family tree.

I never imagined I'd want to speak to my brothers even if it were unexpectedly or because I phoned them: How are you? What's up? But they were never home and never returned my calls. They were my brothers, not some strangers I had accidentally bumped into. We shared a common past even if that didn't matter to them. They couldn't escape it even if they didn't miss me. Often I wondered what they thought: Had they wanted to call me? "Don't worry," Rafael would say. "The moment one of them needs me, he'll suddenly pop up. Why do you want to see them? To put up with your sisters-in-law?"

Maybe in San Lázaro I first became aware of their empty place, their absence, of solitude and time, the changes and the nostalgia of my childhood. Back then I rarely played with dolls. I knew how to win at marbles, push the little cars so they wouldn't go off the highway my brothers painted with white chalk or lime on the sidewalks, to fire a cap pistol to defend my ranch until the Lone Ranger and Tonto arrived to save me or how to keep the soccer ball out of the net so they wouldn't score any goals. For many years the three of us were inseparable. My stepbrothers, on the other hand, occasionally came to visit and, every so often, came with their children to eat at my house. How strange life is, how contradictory: two beings who suddenly appeared to break my mother's heart were now my friends, my allies. We spoke to each other respectfully but not with indifference. It wasn't their fault my father had met their mother at the custom's agency. And though my mother heatedly denied it, I was sure that my father had died in his other wife's house. That's something I wanted to ask my stepbrothers but jealousy held me back because it would be admitting that they not only knew more about my father but that he had favored them. Stupid, I know.

I was as eager to see the photos of my relatives as a bureaucrat waits for a promotion or a bonus, as a father awaits his son's graduation or a mother waits to see her daughter in a wedding dress. It was excitement or happiness, I'm not sure which, finally to find out something about my paternal family. I longed to confirm in the photos my place in the lives of others and to find somewhere my oval face or wide forehead or the slanted eyes and thin lips of my brothers. I'd put together a picture album for my children. I'd leave them a keepsake, a relic that would perhaps mean nothing to them until they were grown-up, a remembrance not passed down to me. My children could then say one day: "We're from here," descendants of men and women with real faces, with authentic traits and facial expressions.

My mother's family—good, peaceful and modest people resigned to life's ups-and-downs—had always lived nearby. My grandparents moved to Mexico City shortly after my mother settled there. And we never knew our grandparents, but my mother not only preserved the family relics, but also her few furnishings, which I eventually added to mine. A sewing machine, a breakfront, a cane chair. But the names, dates and accomplishments of my father's family were not part of my genealogical tree.

All I wanted was to say: "These were the people from whom I inherited my brown hair, hands like father's, my insecurity, nervousness, unstable nature. What's happening is his fault, not mine."

My mother would complain about my brothers: "They inherited Souza genes, Marcela." But when I asked her why they hadn't seen the Souzas ever again, what had they done, she bit her tongue, as if she knew nothing. My mother muffled her tragedy and my father's; and once I learned the truth, it was difficult for me to understand why.

More than anything else, I was looking for distraction or rationalization that would free me from the crime of not feeling any guilt that I wagered on Eduardo's love and lost.

My picture of my paternal family was not idyllic but rather beyond understanding. It was difficult for me to envision them walking down the same clean, cobblestone streets that I went along in the afternoon as the sun was setting. I found it incredible that they had lived in those huge colonial mansions downtown, the ones that barely remained standing, like 57 Hidalgo Street, where my great-grand-parents had died and where my father's cousin—where I was going to lunch—still lived.

The grated windows and the stonework facade would still be there like witnesses of the past. The iron-studded door and the sliding bolts, the wrought iron balconies, the tiled patios and the marble checkerboard floors would still be there though badly worn. In the living room, where I later would sit, and whose windows would be wide open displaying the wealth of former days to all who happened to pass, I would see still hanging there the same rectangular mirror where my great-grandmother had combed her hair and her daughters had admired their dresses and the room filled with wicker furniture where my great grandfather had received his friends. I would see those high ceilings and thick walls that must've borne witness to my grandfather's birth and the excitement of the wedding engagements of his six sisters. Later I'd find out how many they were.

No, it wasn't romanticizing my ancestors. I saw the arrogant women (my mother said: "The Souzas were arrogant") climbing into their horse-drawn carriages wearing uncomfortable dresses or taking the mule-drawn trolley for a ride, or haggling with the Indians over the price of rainwater and arguing with my great-grandfather over the dinner menu for the governor's visit. I could see the men from afar, always in suits in the heat, energetic, keeping an eye on their workers toiling in the heat, arguing over the cost of living, worrying over the rebellious *criollos* and Indians at the same time they subjected the Indian servants to the whims of their children.

I had not talked with my relatives or taken them on a jaunt to the beach or the Bella Vista Ranch or the main square, nor had I rummaged through the trunks of my grandmothers and my aunts. I didn't have to go to hell and back to remember what I hadn't lived. I could make up my family history as I pleased to reinvent myself because I didn't like the real truth. I wasn't what I would have wanted to be. I knew that I had within me a sleeping monster that could wake at any moment and be violent or cruel, disloyal or unfaithful. I was terrified by the knowledge that I was the only one who had felt it.

I was certain that the certificates—the first step to knowing myself—would be found in the Church Archives.

The first Souza we knew of was a sailor named Leandro, just like my father. In 1780 he was the captain of the mailboat *Our Lady of the Light*. We found this out when a friend of my brothers discovered it by accident in the Communications Office of the Veracruz National Public Archives while working for his doctorate on the ship logs which recorded the arrival and departure of ships from Veracruz harbor in the 17th and 18th centuries.

"How was that Souza related to your family?" he asked my brothers.

"Papá, how was he related to us?" I asked. All he answered was: "He must have been a relative."

This was the reference:

The Veracruz Port Superintendent announces the departure to San Lázaro of the mailboat Our Lady of the Light. *The ship captain Leandro Souza did not consign a list of the cargo he was carrying.*

The governor of Veracruz announces the arrival of the mailboat Our Lady of the Light *from San Lázaro. The ship captain Leandro Souza reported having observed English vessels nearby.*

Then in the papers Miguel gave me, I read that that Seaman Souza, a Santa Cruz de Tenerife native, who had seen the English pirates, had stopped going out to sea and built a house to bring back a wife from the Canary Islands. She never made it, having died on the high seas, so he ordered another wife from Mores, in the Kingdom of Aragon, from where his friend Gregorio Zorraquino hailed. This woman arrived pregnant, so instead he finally decided to marry Ramona Sagasti, the illegitimate daughter of Don Ramón Sagasti and Doña Ciriaca Flota of Vizcaya.

You ask me, madam, to describe to you this town where I have ended up and to which I would like you to come. For your religious observance we have the churches of Jesús, Saint Joseph, San Andrés and the church and convent of San Francisco, all very ancient. Running along the sea you will find a row of limestone houses owned by Spaniards. They are pleasing to the eye due to their grillwork, the stonework patterns and the lovely carved doors. Here there are craftsmen very skilled and knowledgeable in these materials and I assure you, madam, that nowhere in your home town will you find furniture such as that which graces our houses, having arrived on boats that have anchored here from all parts of Europe.

And that Souza must have set up his carpentry shop, and his descendants must have become tradesmen and land-owners whose fortune declined as they sent their children to study in Spain, France or the United States, because the young people did not want to work behind a counter or worry about a lack of laborers to work the fields.

So together with what Miguel supplied, I started to shape the history of the Souzas, albeit superficially. Thanks to him, I was ashamed of my great-great grandparents for having exploited the Indians on their corn, rice, sugar cane and dyewood plantations while their naïve and obedient or arrogant and proud women said vespers or novenas or the rosary in the San Andrés Church, the same one whose clang still kept calling the faithful to Mass.

I had no childhood memories of the San Lázaro patron saint festivities, nor of the carnivals, nor the patriotic celebrations in the Malva Theater. Nor do I remember the color of the pitayas or the taste of the zapotes, the taste of the Indian and mestizo cuisine, the fragrance of the flowers, the almond trees, the flamboyant trees, or the night blossoms, or the cries of the children that were born at home, or the agony of those who died of yellow fever or colic. I remembered nothing, not even locked in my dreams. Nothing.

The morning light now entered the room through the gap between the window curtains. I stood up and drew them back. Looking at the bay, I saw the turquoise sea still as a pool. The shrimp boats had gone out and only a few boats and skiffs were scattered here and there, tied to the docks, seagulls their only crew.

There was little movement toward the main square. The clothing, grocery and handicraft shops had not yet opened, but waiters were dragging tables onto the restaurant sidewalks and throwing brightly colored yellow and orange cloths on the tables for the breakfast crowd. The streets were mostly empty, except for the few men who were sweeping the park, and here and there a pedestrian.

I watched the blue and white mosaic cupolas of the San Gabriel and the San Juan churches, and the Indian laurels in the San Fernando Plaza. The starlings had flown off early, like the fishermen. Every once in a while a flock of seagulls would fly across the sky, and a brave gull would dive down into the water for fish.

I walked to my desk and picked up one of the opened letters.

Listening to your voice on the phone, I tried to remember the number of times that I had seen you. I missed the voice that lit up my office, even from the hallway. I had wanted to confess that I desired something more than friendship, but couldn't for fear of frightening you off. What was I doing falling in love with a woman so much younger than myself? I would step into the operating room, thinking of you, Marcela, and I'd walk out with your image at my side. I was no longer Eduardo Carrillo, Elizabeth's father, husband of Ilona Soskay, cardiologist, university professor...Eduardo Carrillo was no longer the hospital director, the doctor, the friend of his friends. Marcela, Eduardo Carrillo was a poor devil in love who now had no past, no future. "Here I am, I thought, after all these years, forced to play different roles."

I would walk out into the streets and gratefully observe people who did not know me, because I didn't need to pretend in front of them. I looked at the gray city sky, and it seemed to me that, contaminated as it was, it filled my life, since it didn't seem to threaten me. You were the house I wanted to inhabit, the room in which I wanted to sleep. With you at my side it was easier for me to play the role of father, husband, doctor, professor. Even at night, it was easier making love to my wife. Does this confession hurt you?

Having you, Marcela, I concluded late in life that the sexual mores of Saint Augustine and Saint Paul were absurd, that their condemnation of the body, pleasure and desire contradicted man's natural instincts. Why such hostility toward pleasure and sexuality? Didn't an angel fight against the forbidden, always the stronger passion? That is why I prefer Abelard's rebellion to all theology. Don't you find Abelard's passion for Heloise marvelous?

And yet as I would realize later, Eduardo followed Saint Paul and Saint Augustine's ethics to a tee.

I was suddenly thirsty. I put down the letter and drank more than half a bottle of distilled water; then I decided to take a shower before going down for breakfast. I don't know how long I stood under the water. I remember that it rushed out, that it was like music enveloping me.

"What was the point of rereading Eduardo's letters?" I asked myself several times. Why then did I put off rereading them? I still hated myself. Why had I written to him in the first place? Why did I agree to have dinner with him that first time? It's amazing how your life can change by simply answering a phone call, by running into someone on a trip or in a doctor's office, by going to a dinner you hadn't planned on attending.

I won't go, I told myself. I won't go. But you end up doing things you hadn't wanted to do. I was nervous going to the San Angel Inn. I was wearing a new dress and new shoes and had cut my hair to feel more elegant, more sure of myself, more stylish or attractive. Things you do which you won't admit to doing. I knew it was a trap for both Eduardo and me; well, I knew I wouldn't have agreed to meet him had I not felt attracted to him, not wanted to seduce him, not felt excited by him.

That afternoon began a new period of my life: days of meeting him for lunch or coffee or walking in the Tlalpan woods lost among the joggers, fat women exercising to lose weight, the elderly stretching their legs to remain limber. Days of feeling different, being someone else, the object of someone else's attention. A time when the absence of my mother and my brothers didn't matter much, when Rafael's job wouldn't compete with me and when my coming home would be a return to the future, since my present had changed. It was a period in which I didn't wake up in the middle of the night or start to cry over nothing.

When I arrived at the San Angel Inn, I waited in the courtyard surrounded by shrubs and lots of hydrangeas, daisies and potted geraniums. My eyes focused on the fountain where red tulips floated on the water as I floated in dreamland. The towering eucalyptus trees were thick with leaves and smelled of forest and the countryside. It was easy to imagine you were not in the city.

People were sitting at the tables in the courtyard. They talked confidently and sipped their drinks or ate appetizers with the ease of people enjoying their home garden sitting under an umbrella. I, on the other hand, felt out of place.

"Why there, Eduardo? We'll run into lots of people we know."

"Precisely. They won't think we are hiding something."

I was jealous of the people who seemed to be enjoying the afternoon. I didn't want to go into the main dining room because I was scared to death. I needed to arm myself with courage: I knew I ran the risk of seeing one of Rafael's friends. I could still run off, yet I went inside.

Eduardo was already there waiting for me at a window table, in full view of everyone. The head waiter led me to him.

"Am I late?" I asked, not knowing what to say or how to greet him.

"You're right on time, Marcela," he answered, standing up.

We shook hands without smiling. We were both clearly nervous. Then I glanced across the room and tried to assume an urbane expression, one of civility and tact. Eduardo had brushed his hair carefully and seemed quite decorous in his navy blue suit and his green and yellow checkered tie. And it was this formality that made him seem unsure of himself: something in his eyes gave him away. He had a serious, reflective expression, perhaps because he wasn't sure what would happen. He didn't appear calm.

I thought that if I weren't there, I'd be at home, waiting for my children to return from school. Today they would eat alone or just nibble on something before running out into the yard to toss the ball into the basket that Pancho had recently attached to a wall. I thought that Rafael could very well come to the restaurant and see me and I didn't have an excuse prepared for him. I also thought that it was foolish to have lied and not told him I was to have lunch with Eduardo.

"Would you like a martini? They're good here," Eduardo finally said.

"No thanks," I replied. "I'll have a tequila."

I needed to get drunk quickly. The bell captain signaled for a waiter to take our order and then disappeared.

The San Angel Inn is an old hacienda in the southern edge of Mexico City; it has a huge garden, but sadly, our window faced the street.

Two or three times our conversation was interrupted. "How are you, doctor? It's a pleasure to see you."

Eduardo acted as if everything was normal; in fact he introduced me openly: "This is Sra. Hernández."

I am Sra. Her-nán-dez. Marcela Souza de Hernández. Hernández. Oh my God!

As time went by, Eduardo appeared happy but a bit cautious, as if he had been thinking: "Finally! But I must be careful not to scare her off." He smoked, though he was a cardiologist who recommended that his patients give up the vice; his nostrils flared, making his face appear sharp, intense. I watched his hands. They were long and bony, so tanned one would've thought he was out in the sun most of the time. Eduardo stayed holed up in his office or in the hospital, but later I found out that he would spend weekends in his Cuernavaca home. Still neither his hands nor his face had the typical age spots of older people. I looked at him to memorize him: bushy eyebrows, brown eyes, straight nose, thick lips.

I felt like a dimwit. I had waited anxiously for that meeting and now couldn't speak: it was as if I were only waiting for him to speak. The tequila loosened me up just a bit.

Our short and fat waiter was very polite. "What would you like as a main course, Miss? At your service, Doctor."

"Miss," I thought. He had stressed, without mentioning it directly, the difference in our ages. "Miss." I wanted to spin around and say something awful to him like "midget" or "fatso," just to see the expression on his face when I said it.

The conversation with Eduardo relaxed me again, made me forget where I was—in view of the entire world. I began to feel better and forget the polite words the waiter had used. It was like explaining to your easygoing professor that you hadn't had the chance to study for the final. He would understand.

After a silence, Eduardo said: "No one has ever caressed me with a letter before, Marcela."

"I wanted to know you, but I was afraid to see you," I answered.

"Can we talk openly?"

I nodded. It was strange, because at once Eduardo stopped being Dr. Carrillo and immediately entered into my confidence. I looked toward the window; Dr. Carrillo, was on the outside, killed off by my mother's death. "I didn't follow you, I didn't pursue you, I didn't desire you." I wanted to apologize.

"Why wouldn't you speak to me?"

"I told you already. I was afraid."

"You're beautiful, Marcela." This made me blush.

I picked up my napkin. "I like your letters."

"I like to look at you."

"Will you continue to write to me?"

"Will I continue to see you?"

I spoke as if trying to remember an address or phone number I had forgotten. I stuttered, but Eduardo calmed me down. "I don't know which of us is more nervous. I feel like a teenager again."

I laughed. "That's what the actors in soap operas my mother watched said: 'You're beautiful,' 'I feel like a teenager again.'"

"I'm being corny," he said, upset.

I didn't want to humiliate him, but I wasn't used to those kinds of comments. Rafael never said those things, nothing at all like that. I'm not complaining. He has other ways to tell me when I please him: the way he winks or puts his arm around me.

The conversation was all about me. Eduardo questioned me about my job at the ad agency where I arrived every morning to sit in front of a desk to squeeze out ideas until any old product became a *necessity* for the consumer, and then I'd convert my ideas into images. Though it's deceptive and base, I enjoy my job, it amuses me. After all, I spend my time inventing Aladdin's lamps, rubbing them so that the client or the consumer imagines the genie coming out.

The wine livened me up, and I went on answering his questions, not avoiding telling him about my children and Rafael. I had never imagined I would have two sons. It was easier for me to imagine having two disobedient or unmanageable girls. I had to deal with soccer, karate, bloody noses, not wanting to study, even the fighting between them. I don't know who they're like because they don't resemble Rafael or me. Maybe they're pure Souza.

The boys would be going off to England in a few months. The youngest, who is clever and smart, started falling off in school after my mother's death. We were getting called in all the time: he wasn't studying, he had a bad attitude, he wouldn't cooperate with his classmates, and so on. Rafael decided he should study abroad for a year and settle down. The eldest also wanted to go, and it seemed a good idea for them to be together, especially since they would learn English. Rafael speaks it and I know it so-so because English interested me and I paid attention in school. I don't really master anything.

While I talked, Eduardo carefully observed me, as if he wanted to know what I thought of him, if I considered him corny or daring, bold or ridiculous. Truth was that what most attracted me to him was that I didn't know him, that he was a secret I would discover in time. Yes, I suppose it was that, to know one another, which was the source of nervousness for us both. It was as if we were reading the same novel and wanted to reach the end very slowly, or we were listening to the same music and were dying to have the score in hand so we could follow it at our leisure. Desire increased within both of us with each passing word.

When Eduardo accompanied me to my car, he stood right in front of me and held my hand; he took out a small wooden box from his pant's pocket. Looking at me playfully and suggestively, he said good-bye. "It's not a letter, Marcela. It's a gift for your game. Please call me whenever you feel like seeing me. I'll be waiting."

I didn't call him though that night, and for many nights after I could still feel the exact spot where he pressed my hand. I told myself over and over that I had done the right thing, that it had been worth it to eat with Dr. Carrillo, but each time the phone rang in my office, I would suddenly give a start.

I don't know how many times I reread his letters, the sheets, folded four ways, that were in the box. Thirty in all. Thoughts that lovers have and very often never say.

How happy I was unfolding and reading each and every one of them. That's when I realized I was truly in love with Eduardo.

- *I think of you many times during the day.*
- *What lies beyond your gaze, Marcela?*
- *I would like to take your hand gently and fly off with you.*
- *I dream about the day I can hold you for ten seconds, just ten seconds (I don't know how or when) curled up in my arms.*
- *I am going to tell you a secret: I love you.*

How can someone capable of expressing such things turn into such a coward?

Chapter Five

I was having breakfast when I heard my name on the loud-speaker. Someone was paging me. I got up and went to the telephone at the front desk.

"Who is it?" I asked.

"Why didn't you call me last night?"

"I fell asleep."

"How are you?"

"Pretty well. Feeling hot." I was trying to be kind.

You try kindness whenever you feel guilty about something: the secretary who forgot to make the urgent call you asked her to make, the assistant who manages the petty cash box at his discretion, the taxi-driver who speeds up his meter. It's a way to ease your bad conscience.

"Are you really well? I think it's crazy for you to be there."

I said nothing. If it were crazy, what could I say? That he was right?

"A letter came from your sons."

Your sons is how he said it, but he hadn't meant to put them down, it was just a way to make me feel important.

"What do they say?"

"They're happy, it's cold there...Not much else, you know what they're like."

"Being happy is the most important thing, no? Do you really think they're happy?"

I certainly missed them...probably more than I was willing to admit. I pretended to be strong, but I missed their uproar, their surprise at the world they were discovering and making the most of.

"Sure, I already told you they were."

"Can you read me their letter?"

"I left it at home and I'm at the office. What are your plans?"

"I'm going to the city archives and then to my father's cousin's house. I guess I'll have dinner there. I'll tell you about it later. Let me call you tonight."

"Okay—"

"Rafael, how are you?" I broke in because I was anxious to know.

"Loaded with work," he answered as usual. "I send you a kiss." He hung up.

Back at the table, I realized that I had to accept that Rafael, after all, was a good husband. And I was ungrateful. I had little to complain about except that he was in his own world, and because I was not in it, it was easy for me to slip away from him. But that's how he is, how he's always been. An ambitious man, used to thinking that he's always right. Like a good lawyer, he knows how to turn everything around.

"How can you defend that guy?"

"It's what I do."

And he studies his cases to the most minute detail and if he finds any loophole, he makes sure his client wins. That's why everyone wants him. It's not my business to judge if this is good or bad. As he says, it's what he does.

Perhaps the first thing I liked about him was his boldfaced ambition. I compared him to my father, a conformist, a man who never lifted a finger to improve himself. He did his work and went home (I don't know to which of his two homes he went first), and this continues to be a problem for me. It's amazing that we didn't suspect anything. My mother must have resisted believing it, then probably hated it, but she never said a word. That's how she was, incapable of thinking she had any other lot in life.

Rafael's passion is his office, his clients, his cases. He

believes that economic stability is the most important thing for the family. Wouldn't it be better if he spent more time with them? And if he has had a romance, a love affair, I've not been aware of it and don't know how I would react. I never expect anything from him, for him to notice that I dyed my hair or put on a new dress. He lives in his own world, yes, but what would I throw in his face? His love of work? He stumbled into something that I have yet to find. All I have is a series of frustrations. Music, for example, is one of my many frustrations, though I enjoy it. Listening to Mendelssohn's *Song of the Gondolier* is not the same thing as playing it and I don't play it not because I don't feel like it ("Just excuses," my father used to say, "You haven't even tried"), but because I truly wasn't born for it. If I displayed technique, my teacher would ask why I played with such little feeling; if I played with feeling, she'd ask me what had happened to the technique.

I sat down at a table and drank my coffee while watching a waiter observing the breasts of one customer and the legs of another in shorts. I looked all around the restaurant for the couple who had played the same song over and over the night before, but didn't see them. Maybe they have taken a tour of the ruins, maybe they were in the swimming pool or still in their room. Who knows? "If they put on the same song again tonight, I'm going to complain to the manager," I swore, not because the lyrics weren't beautiful or the music nice, but because it disturbed me and kept me from being alone with myself.

I put the paper in front of me and read while eating. The news featured only the political developments in the country and in San Lázaro. The investigations into the Colosio affair, the Ruiz Massieu case, Comandante Marcos's public statements, the struggle for power among the various political parties, the governor's speech at public works ceremonies. The society section was rather thick while a single article on an assault constituted the crime page. The language in the society articles was depressing: "The gorgeous young lady"—and the overall design of the paper, third class.

When I had finished breakfast, I went up to my room to brush my teeth and take up Eduardo's letters again. I didn't want to leave them; holding them gave me some kind of security, as if they were amulets. I felt that I could stop somewhere, and reread them.

I walked out of the hotel and stuck my face into the open doorways, not worried about dogs since I had discovered there wasn't a single one in the downtown area. Some women swept the courtyards while others cleaned the cages of their canaries or parakeets—jabbering parrots as they're called in San Lázaro—while still others watered mimosa, jasmine and *coralillo* flowerpots.

I gasped for breath; the humidity rose as the morning heat increased. A strong odor of salt and fish floated in the air, perhaps coming from the shrimp packers. As I went along, I'd look into the shop windows which at some point must have been dyewood warehouses or the rooms of huge mansions where obviously the owners no longer lived. I couldn't say how or how much the city had changed since this was my first trip to it. I didn't fill a prescription at the pharmacist's or pick up a bag of honey caramel from the candy store, or visit the carpenter so he could build me a chair or a table. I didn't know who lived in the houses or ran the businesses downtown or to whom they had been sold or who had inherited them. Those mansions had a history meaningful to San Lázaro's residents, but not to tourists. Still I was surprised by the large number of abandoned houses; I later found out from Miguel that this was because no will had been left or because the heirs lacked the money to repair them. You could see the undergrowth creeping up to the once shuttered windows, and the wooden doors were half-eaten by humidity and wood lice. I was scared of losing my way along the unfamiliar streets or narrow alleyways.

I compared the prices with those in Mexico City and everything—for example, the green hardbound notebook I bought in a stationery store to jot down my findings at the archives—seemed more expensive.

I lingered for a while on Juárez Street because from it you could see the archway leading to the port as well as the one going inland. Years back these had been the only entrances into the walled city. As time passed, other gates were added and finally whole sections of the wall were demolished for the trolleys or to make it easier for cars to enter or to improve the access to a particular avenue.

I walked on calmly yet bothered by the humidity now clinging to my body. Then I heard a piano. The music was coming from a window. I drew near and saw a young man playing a Mozart sonata. I stood there, listening to him run through the piece twice. It seemed odd for someone to be playing Mozart at that time and place. The piano was a Petrof or old Weinbach upright, I really couldn't tell for sure. I'd have given anything to have one like that as a teenager. The young man stopped playing at the same place and would just start over. What was he doing playing Mozart at nine in the morning?

"Good morning," he said when he discovered me. He didn't look at me.

"I love Mozart," I replied, "it's his *Sonata in*—"

"*E Flat.*"

So sad and delicate, so sweet and melancholy, it makes you feel like crying.

Perhaps I repeat myself, but I owe my fondness for music to my father. It was his favorite pastime. And perhaps because he played piano as a child but never told me—he was no musician—he enrolled me in the National School of Music. But I never achieved the success he had expected; still, music was a part of my life. It took him years to accept that I didn't have a musical calling.

"I once tried to learn it."

"Uh huh," he said, still not looking.

He didn't want to waste his time on me and I understood.

Walking down the San Lázaro streets I felt free and independent; this made me feel good. For some reason, I didn't have to push myself to face life there. Maybe the blue sky and sun were making me happy.

I finally reached San Andrés. I entered along one side, by the atrium, and asked a man with a priestly air sitting in an office what was needed to look through the archives.

"You need permission," he said, examining me.

"Whose?"

"The archbishop's."

"How can I get it?"

"Are you a researcher?" he asked me doubtfully.

"Yes," I replied. After all, I wasn't really lying, though it's a habit I've easily picked up.

"What are you looking for?" he asked, changing tone.

"The birth, baptism, and death certificates of my grandparents and great-grandparents. They must be here."

"Or in the Civil Register," he corrected.

"Maybe."

"Do you know from when?"

"More or less."

"Hmmm."

"Can I look them up?"

"Access to the archives is restricted because of their present state. I've already told you that you need permission and it's almost impossible to get it. I'm sorry."

"Please—"

"I can't help you."

"Please," I repeated.

"Look," he explained. "Let me show you."

He opened a door. Out rushed a dampness that struck my face; the stench of old paper invaded my nostrils. I saw two fans and several bookcases filled with cardboard boxes.

The bound certificates were falling apart, that much was clear. I had imagined sitting in front of a computer screen looking through microfilm.

"Why are the files in that condition?"

"That's precisely why access to them is restricted."

How would I find anything if I couldn't prove I was a researcher?

"Which family are you researching?"

"The Souzas. Do you know anything about them?"

"Whose daughter are you?"

"You need to create an artificial climate. Someone has to put everything on microfilm before it vanishes."

"And you're going to pay for it?" he said angrily.

I kept quiet. My tactlessness was endangering my access to the books.

"I'm the daughter of Leandro Marcelo Souza, husband of Dolores Sierra from Tabasco. My father moved away soon after he married and never saw his family again. I want to research them. Please help me."

"Only if you can provide the correct dates. Go to the Municipal Library and look through the biographical dictionaries. The Souzas have been in this state for many generations and you'll be sure to find information to help us."

He said "help us," and I realized he was kinder than I had initially thought. He was tall and thin, with dark hair falling over a large head. He wore khaki pants and a checkered shirt and had green, transparent eyes.

"What about the permission?"

"You can pay one of the people working here. If you're not a researcher, you cannot come in," he said ironically.

"And your name, sir?"

"Juan Buenfil. Father Buenfil."

"Thank you," I said. "I'm going to the library. I hadn't thought of going there."

"If you find something, ask for Sra. Canto, the director, when you come back. She should be here soon."

"Father Buenfil," I repeated out on the streets. "Father Buenfil and Sra. Canto" I wrote down in my notebook.

People casually walked by me, laughing. I turned down Madero to pass once more the house where the young man played the piano. He kept practicing the same notes, but at another section of the piece. I know what that's like. Still he had talent, you could tell at once.

Miguel told me later that many musicians from the National University Orchestra and the Orchestra of Jalapa were from San Lázaro.

"It's something common to hear children playing piano all over the city every afternoon," he went on. "It's a tradition. We have good teachers. Then the students go off, continuing their studies somewhere else. That's also part of the tradition."

I went into the library; it was full of people. Most were students. The window facing the street was wide open and the room was suffused with light. On the walls, however, you could see salt and mildew. I got in the information line and patiently waited for my turn.

I had been so stupid; it had never occurred to me to look for my relatives in an encyclopedia or a historical or biographical dictionary. Actually, I didn't think any of them would be there. Moreover, my mother's family wouldn't be in the Tabasco telephone directory because they were from a village far off from the capital.

It was easier than I had expected. In the *Biographical and Historical Dictionary of San Lázaro*, I found my unknown great grandfather's biography:

Descended from an ancient family lineage, Don Santiago Souza came into the world in the city and port of San Lázaro the first of May, 1832...He completed his law studies at the Lazarine Institute, then moved to Jalapa, Veracruz to take his final exams in fulfillment of the Justice Administration Law degree...He married María del Carmen Cálcena in 1858...

It was an official biographical note which I copied in my green notebook, just below where I had put the names of the Archive directors. The citation was in flowery, but official, language much like textbook biographies: *they procreated twelve children.* I found out that my great-grandfather had owned three haciendas: Santiago, Homol, and La Azucena. He died at age 65, on September 25th, 1897.

Naturally, I did not find a single line about my great-grandmother. Who is going to write about women given over to raising children?

What had María del Carmen Cálcena's life been like? I guessed that perhaps she had been the daughter of conservative Spaniards whose character and pleasures were not different from those of her husband. That's how it may have been, why not? Perhaps she had left her parent's hacienda, the luxury, the trips to Havana, just to end up giving birth to one child after the other. Twelve children, according to the dictionary. One by one they must have sapped her strength.

I'd have liked to know how she had fallen in love with my great-grandfather and how women of that period kept hidden, in such a small place, their secret affairs.

I found nothing on my grandparents.

I went back to the Archbishop's Archives and found Sra. Canto. It had to be her. Short, thin, light-complexioned, and with green eyes like those of Father Buenfil. Her reading glasses hung down on a chain in front of her.

"Are you Sra. Canto?"

"How can I help you," she said in a friendly voice.

"I stopped by several hours ago. Father Buenfil said you could help me. I want to know if—"

"Fill out this form," she interrupted.

Later I found out that Sra. Canto had studied anthropology in Mexico City and had her Masters in Archival Studies. Since returning to San Lázaro she had struggled to restore the archives. She knew them like the back of her hand.

"This is all the info I have," I told her. "But if you find any other certificate that mentions my family, please..."

"Do you want to make a family tree?"

"Not exactly. I only want to know who my ancestors were. What their names were, where they came from. My father never spoke of anyone. It's strange not knowing where you come from."

"Where do you come from?"

"I told you I don't know."

"From Mexico City?"

"Yes, from there. I'm staying at the Hotel Fénix."

"You don't have any relatives here?"

"Distant relatives, but I don't know them. I'm going to visit some uncles—"

"Come back tomorrow at this time," she said, dismissing me. "We will have to charge you for the transcription." She turned her head and shouted: "Julio, come here, sweetie. I got a little job that'll keep you busy for a while."

Chapter Six

It was as if I had closed a window and once more my distant past had stayed outside, floating free. Only my recent past came back to me. I thought of going to a park bench to read Eduardo's letters, but after a few minutes of walking outside, the heat changed my mind. I was dying of thirst, so I went into one of the restaurants on the main square.

I sat in a corner, under a fan, and ordered an ice-cold Corona. The aroma of the food cooking made me recall my mother's kitchen, where I had been so happy. My family usually gathered in the kitchen—that's where my mother could generally be found. We'd sit around the table and discuss trivial or important things. My brother Alberto walked in there showing off the first suit he'd bought with his first paycheck. He modeled it, waiting for our approval. I remember its wide lapels which mom hadn't liked; it was too chic, and would soon be out-of-style and worthless to him. My mother was a bit conservative and frightened by what was "in"; yet she was partly right, for Alberto looked a bit odd in that suit which hadn't been tailored to fit him.

When we were kids, mother would dress us for school in the kitchen in the winter. She'd open the oven door so we wouldn't shiver from the cold or she'd pour alcohol in a bucket and light it with a match so it would burn while we dressed.

The smells that emerged from my mother's pots were different than those in other houses, and I associate happiness and human contact with those odors. She'd go on foot to the market carrying a wicker basket and return accompanied by a small boy who helped her carry it back to the kitchen.

"Don't be in such a rush, child," she would say to him. "Let me get you something to eat."

And so we'd find him working busily, taking oranges, serrano peppers, coriander, bay leaves, tomatoes, onions, little packages of black pepper and oregano, meat or fish wrapped in wax paper, and vegetables out of the basket...while my mother made tacos because she knew that the boy only had a jugful of sugared coffee in his stomach.

I'd see my mother in her checkered apron, with her pockets weighed down by her keys.

It wasn't only the unique smells and tastes that made our kitchen different. She herself was different, eagerly cooking for us because she wasn't undertaking something forced on her or a boring chore but a rite of which she was proud, one that wasn't a burden. Cooking, sewing, fearing my father were the only things that came naturally to her. May she forgive me.

If I'm indebted to my father for my love of music, I owe my love of cooking to my mother. My girlfriends grumble, but I enjoy choosing ingredients for my dishes, mixing them together, playing in that lab where you can concoct, experiment, try out, feel your way through the process. Like her, I pamper my children, delight friends and please Rafael through my cooking.

There was a black clay vase filled with rare, exotic flowers on the table. Yellow and purple, they smelled of jungle, of the tropics. I asked the waiter what they were when he served my Corona in a frosted mug.

"Balsam and allamanda flowers," he said, as if reciting a poem.

I had a sip of beer and took Eduardo's letters out of my purse. What choice did I have? I randomly picked one out, I'd have liked to tell a friend: "Listen to this."

Marcela, I come to you after having crossed such a wide expanse that I feel tired of my very being. You question me about my past when I'm at the point where what's happened says nothing about my true self, where I've gone forward without reassessing it. We Mexicans are overly prone to talk about the past, to reevaluate it so as to define ourselves from that point on. If you think I'm wrong, look over our main cultural developments from the 19th century on.

Sometimes our past is of such little value that it can deceive us when we don't find anything worth remembering. I think that everyone should be capable of freeing himself from the past, at least that's what I've tried to do.

He addressed me in the familiar "tu" form, closing the distance of our previous meeting, as he had suggested at the San Angel Inn. But it wasn't easy for me to use the "tu" form: it was a question of how I was raised. I used the "usted" form, not to create a distance between us but out of respect. In my house we used the formal to address a teacher, a doctor, our godfather. I had admired Eduardo from the start because of his reputation, his profession, his age, and because, of course, he was my mother's doctor. At first I thought of Eduardo always in a formal way. I had written in my notebook:

I don't know my past. How can I free myself from it? When you don't know it, the past makes you as uneasy as the future. Where's my future heading? Nowhere, it seems.

I went on reading:

Marcela, you tell me about your childhood as innocently as someone who has just left it. Your portrait of your father is severe. You're unfair, I think. I dare to think it. Let me say that maybe your father wasn't ambitious, a virtue rarely found in this world. People like him are happier than you can imagine.

He must've used music and literature to rise above his frustrations. Who wouldn't want that?

But Eduardo made no mention of my father's other family.

As to your brothers' absence, I have little to say. Didn't your father do the same thing? Didn't he also leave his home behind? "You will leave your father and your mother…"

I'm starting to appreciate the way you invent or see yourself. Women always talk about their childhood to define themselves. It's not that I think that's wrong, Marcela. Simply put, other things define me…friends, for example. Friendship is sacred. In this awful world a friend in whom you can confide is a blessing, don't you agree? I am also defined by my profession (I suppose I needn't go into details about that, since it's a part of me you know well), my patients (who your patients are says a lot about you), and the women I've loved (had I only met you earlier…).

I'm defined by my reading. I prefer Conrad by far to other writers, but I have a certain weakness for Greene because I share not only his anguish over faith, but also over guilt. Just consider how he makes so many of his characters come alive; but that might not interest you much. A woman like you, Marcela, who questions me in such an unusual way probably doesn't know much about guilt and hopefully you'll escape remorse. Remorse is not enough. No, not if you don't realize you have to struggle against guilt.

Who doesn't know about guilt and remorse! I would've wanted to ask the waiter if he hadn't trodden that same ground. He was a short and gray-haired bony man full of life. He brought me another frosted mug for my already warm bottled beer.

"From your family?" he asked, referring to the letter.

"From a friend," I replied.

"Well, that's better. Enjoy it."

"Yes," I said, not knowing why, and went on reading.

The music I like also defines me: Mahler, for example, if conducted by Bernstein, so much the better; and my books: those boring things—Congenital Cardiopathy, The History of Cardiology in Mexico, *or the biography of my teacher, Dr. Chávez,* An Overview of a Paradoxical Man—*that no one but a doctor would read.*

My mistakes and my choices during the course of my life define me. The suits I wear define me (I prefer dark colors and hate synthetics), the store where I purchase them (please excuse the pretension and arrogance, but it's been ages since I've worn anything but imported clothes. Not only does imported cloth last longer, but the style, no matter how simple, makes one look distinguished), the cigarette brand I smoke (I who forbid smoking!), my dislike for lotions in general...things like that, Marcela, as simple and ordinary as the food one eats.

Still I am going to be polite: you established the rules of the game and I have accepted them. Here are the answers to your questions:

It's difficult for me to remember my first childhood memory. It was a sound: the hooves of my grandfather Ignacio Carrillo's horse clopping the cobblestones on the main street of my village, as he headed toward my parents' house.

It's nearly dawn. I know that grandfather has come to take me to the fields despite my mother's displeasure. As soon as light enters my room, I put on my pants and shoes, button my shirt, while I race to the doorway to wait for him so he needn't dismount. He lifts me into the air and drops me down on the flank of Duende, the dark chestnut mare he just purchased from Isidro Fabela's father who would later become governor of the State of Mexico, around 1942.

My grandfather eyes me curiously. I ask myself what's he thinking as he covers me with a wool serape that he unfurls from the front of the western saddle so I won't feel the icy air as Duende gallops off.

That's my first childhood memory, Marcela. Not of my parents. It's that bracing authority who marks the dawn in my village. He who comes to teach me to love the countryside, since as the firstborn of the firstborn I will inherit the hacienda; my father, nearsighted and shy about giving orders, was not interested and became a teacher instead.

Village schoolteacher, that was my father. Proud of himself and his profession, not impressed by my grandfather's wealth. Honest and simple as a good village schoolteacher who admired Cato's virtues so much that he chose suicide over living under tyranny.

Marcela, how wrong Don Ignacio Carrillo was. There was something arrogant—did it make me feel important?—about how much I loved those early mornings: to inhale the country smells, to see a valley at my feet and have the peasants take off their hats to greet grandfather, to receive the rising sun that silenced the dark yelping threatening the safety of my dreams. I always knew that I would be leaving there, Marcela, and that my grandfather wouldn't give me up so easily.

When I became a teenager, the first thing I did was to break free from my grandfather's tyranny—I had a good teacher in my father—and from the monotony of those lands where nothing more special occurred than the harvest, the celebration and procession of St. John the Baptist, and St. Isidro Labrador with his March of the Crazies (just peasants in costumes, pulling their oxen decorated with patterned mosaics made of seeds, passing out corn and bean snacks as they went along).

Don Ignacio had a pulque hacienda in Metepec, a freezing village in the Toluca Valley, whose one jewel is still the colonial San Francisco Convent with its cloister of split arches, wooden railings of the choir and the Baroque facade that was added sometime later.

We once went to Metepec and Eduardo showed me not only his parents' house, but also the trails he would take on horseback and what had at one time been his grandfather's hacienda. Nonetheless, he seemed proud of it all. We walked down the narrow roads, with their high embankments, and he'd tell me things like: "Here's where the stove coal was sold, that was the butcher shop, over there the bar…" He took me by the hand as if he wanted not to show me the place but to touch base with his childhood. I remember asking him that morning, a Tuesday we had both taken off from work:

"How much do you love me?"

"From here"—we were sitting on a hill—"to where the village ends. Can you see that far?"

Metepec, the cactus-growing village famous for its Tree of Life molded from clay by the dry hands of its artisans, was my cradle. I was born there, in 1934, and never, Marcela, have I told this story:

My unfortunate grandfather thought he descended from an Andalucian Carrillo and he repeated all his life that he would travel to Spain to meet the family he still had there. When in 1960 I read Angel María Garibay's Spanish version of the Metepec Codices, I was surprised to discover my true origins:

I'm descended not from a Conquistador but from an Indian from the village of Santiago Tlatelolco. This Indian conquered three San Juan Bautista Metepec districts—Santa Margarita, San Bernardo and San Simón—the lands belonging to grandfather's ancestors. It's no coincidence that his hacienda is called San Bernardino.

So that Indian, my forebear, was one of the founders of Metepec. Don Ignacio's arrogance would not have allowed him to know that his last name had more to with the ingenuity of the people than a conquistador's noble lineage.

Garibay translates—this I believe is the root of my last name—that Don Juan Ignacio Xacatzin, the Indian lord from

Santiago Tlatelolco, built a car to carry the "Divine Mystery" to the town church on the day that the first mass was to be celebrated in the village. On his way there the people cheered him loudly "Long Live Don Ignacio and his car!" "Thus Carrillo," the codice clearly states.

One day I told Garibay that, thanks to his paleographic work and his translation of the Metepec Codices, *I was able to complete my family tree down to the 16th Century. And even if not true, I think that that version, which would have killed grandfather, is marvelous.*

How strange, I thought, that Eduardo Carrillo had also researched his origins. I would no longer be able to share with him the results of Sra. Canto's certificate search in the archives. I crossed my fingers somewhat superstitiously and said: "If she finds one I'll be satisfied." I ordered another Corona and went back to the letter, the heat and the commotion growing in the streets. I could see the park from where I sat: it seemed as if the whole town had decided to seek shelter from the sun in the shade of the flamboyant and quebracho trees bursting with red and white flowers.

As I mentioned, Marcela, my father was a teacher. My mother was a teacher as well. She'd recite classic tales, and he taught me Latin, which at that time was required like spelling in the schools. My mother lulled me to sleep with The Golden Ass *and I fell in love with a village girl barely older than me. Her name was Micaela and I considered her more beautiful than Princess Psyche.*

I owe to my mother my obsession with deciphering names, researching their etymology (Marcelo, derived from Marcos, originally Martikos, devotee of Mars. Hence, Marcela, the warrior maiden). Her name was Ana, Christ's grandmother, and that's how she played with me, as if from the other world. "I command you, son, I who was an article of faith, Anatha in Syria and Anat in Canaan. I command you, I who was the bicephalous, two-headed goddess of Time—one head named Prorsa and the other Postverta—to guard the one door to heaven. I command you, I who am the Alpha and Omega, the beginning and the end," and then she would tickle me and overcome my resistance immediately.

My father told me about Caesar's life as if he were relating anecdotes about his brother, and about Achilles' deeds as if he himself had witnessed them. He also told me about Mexico City, where he had gotten his teaching license and had met my mother, a native of Puebla. He was a married man when he came back to Metepec. Grandmother forgave him while grandfather grew bitter.

My parents were loved in Metepec while grandfather was eyed with suspicion because of his wealth. My parents struggled against ignorance and weaned the natives off of pulque while grandfather whipped his workers and cultivated maguey to exploit them further.

I didn't live long with my parents, but this wasn't so odd; if you wanted to get ahead, you had to study in Toluca or Mexico City, and I preferred the latter.

My parents were happy people. They danced in their bedroom to the music on WXEW (they preferred Dámaso Pérez Prado. Do you know his "Mambo #8" or the "Braggart's Mambo"? These were their favorites). My mother washed or cooked singing the songs of Consuelito Velásquez and María Greever: "Promise Me," "Bésame Mucho," "You Said You Loved Me"…See, you've made me remember.

I was jealous of how my father made my mother laugh with his tricks, and I would interrupt their dancing till my mother picked me up and danced to the music, happy with me in her arms.

In Mexico City I ended up dancing and singing to the American Big Bands in style back then: Glenn Miller, Harry James, Billie May, Jimmy Dorsey.

From Ignacio Carrillo I inherited impulsiveness and passion for women. After my grandmother Isidra Sánchez, he *had three other women, each with house and children in town. My grandmother left him and returned to her parents' house in Santiago Tianguistenco. Later on she went to live with a doctor and bore him three daughters. I would go visit her with my father; that's when my interest in medicine began.*

People in Metepec claimed that all the fatherless children were Carrillos. Without boasting, I can honestly say that I was the favorite of all grandfather's offspring to the point that he never spoke to me again once I had decided to continue my studies in Mexico City. He preferred selling the hacienda or parceling it out to the workers to my inheriting it. We never received any of his fortune; all I have of my father's is the certificate naming him Teacher of Metepec, a village I never visited again.

I was still so thirsty that I gulped down the rest of my beer, my mind a blank. I had tossed my distant past out the window, and now I wanted to throw out my recent past. "God almighty," I thought. "How did I let this happen?"

Chapter Seven

I was driving down a sloping road that had so many curves it was as if I were winding down a narrow hill. There was mud and boulders from landslides on one side and a threatening precipice on the other. I wasn't that worried about getting to where I was going—though I didn't know where that place was—because there were other cars in front of me. I figured if they could make it, so could I. What most frightened me was wondering how I could get back; the drive up would be very steep and I was afraid of tumbling over the cliff. I was so scared that I woke up.

I couldn't fall back asleep, so I got up to jot down the dream in my green notebook where I recorded everything, even this story. I was in a bad mood, feeling like a shriveled prune or a bitter lemon: it wasn't hard for me to figure out what the nightmare meant because my planned visit to my father's relatives' house had churned my stomach.

I arrived at 2 p.m., soaked in sweat because the heat in San Lázaro at that time of day is unbearable. Uncle Santiago was in a tee-shirt and Aunt Josefa shouted from the kitchen: "I'm coming, sweetie, I'm coming." There was a sorrowful or abandoned sadness in the air and an intolerable odor of mildew. Despite the summer sun, the house seemed dark and gloomy. My aunt came out of the kitchen perspiring, her hair in a messy white bun, wearing some old slippers that seemed very comfortable on her feet. She was too fat for her age and much too nervous. My uncle observed me with interest and curiosity, as if searching my eyes for my father's.

Before eating, we went into the living room where they offered me a cashew drink. I asked for a Corona instead; this made my uncle happy. The son of my grandfather's brother, he must have been well past ninety. I looked at him warily; he was shriveled up but had blue eyes like my father. He also had a big nose, thin lips and was half deaf. He'd answer "Yes, girl, no, girl" as if he had known me from childhood. And I was amazed by his sharp mind and the agility with which he walked from one side of the house to the other without a cane.

I asked them for a tour of the house. It was huge, with six bedrooms one right after the other, and an office (my uncle had been a notary), but the house was in ruins just like their heritage. The doors to the bedrooms were made of fine wood with beveled glass panes. In the courtyard there was a well still in use with a gargoyle-shaped iron fixture from which hung the chain and the bucket for raising water. Around the well there were flowerpots with roses. In a corner, sweet limes fell from a tree, smelling of citrus blossoms.

The bedroom furniture was antique, but according to my aunt, had not belonged to the family since the old furniture had been divided up except for the living-room rockers where she and her husband would rock back and forth all the time like children. I sat in a chair and listened to them as if I weren't in my own body, but in a story, in a dream. I didn't know what to say because I had nothing to say. It was awful. Of course, they asked about my father, my mother and my brothers.

"Your father was quite handsome," my uncle said. "We were about the same age. I don't remember who was older. But he got it into his head to marry your mother. On a whim."

"I don't understand," I said. "What do you mean?" I used the "usted" form because he was elderly and someone I didn't really know. "On a whim?"

"I thought you knew," my uncle said, sipping his beer nervously.

"Knew what?"

"I think I've said something I shouldn't have."

"Well, you already did, so better let it all out."

I didn't know if I wanted to find out. I was unsure because I sensed it was something painful.

My uncle took another sip of his beer, a longer one, and my aunt seized the opportunity to speak. She wanted to change subjects or somehow delay it.

"Why did you come alone? We would have liked to meet your husband."

I said nothing. I knew my uncle would go on, whether my aunt liked it or not.

"Your grandparents didn't like your mother because she was from a class—"

"For God's sakes, Manuel," my aunt exclaimed.

"My father married against his parents' wishes?"

"They offered him everything under the sun if he wouldn't... You might not know this, but your mother had worked in the kitchen of my uncle's house. That was too much for your grandfather. There were so many upper-class girls to choose from but..."

"Your mother helped around—," my aunt interrupted.

"What do you mean?"

"She was a maid. It's better if you know the truth; I don't know why we adults hide it. There's nothing wrong with it. Your mother was a pretty, happy girl."

At last I could understand my father's silence, a silence that had completely wiped out his family. And I admired my mother even more, because she never spoke ill—truly ill—of any Souza. I felt anger and sadness.

"So they didn't accept my mother?"

"That's how my uncle—your grandfather—was. He wanted your father to take over the business, but he wouldn't be helped by a woman who was..."

"…a maid. Why not say it?"

He held his tongue. He was embarrassed, but satisfied.

"And my father's brothers? Why didn't he see them again?"

"I don't know."

"How many brothers did he have?"

"I can't believe he never spoke about my cousins to his children," he grumbled.

"Not a word."

"There were three: your father, the eldest, and your Uncle Antonio who died as a lad while hunting. They say that his rifle simply went off. And your Aunt Serafina who never married and died in her forties. Isn't that right, Josefa?" he asked his wife.

My aunt said nothing, not even acknowledging the comment.

"Your Aunt Serafina didn't have the courage to stand up to your grandparents. That's why she never married."

"That's what you think!" my aunt said.

My resentment intensified as the facts became clear. My father, so full of himself, so ungiving, so set in his ways. Why hadn't he told us the truth? To protect our mother? To protect our grandparents from our disgust?

My father didn't finish the studies he had begun in San Lázaro. When he arrived in Mexico City, a friend found him a job in the Pasquel Brothers Customs Agency, where he ended his days. He was dependable, as far as work went. Tall, half-bald, thin, and with a mustache, he took my brothers to school early and when he came back from work, he told mother how his day had been, shouting from one room to the other if necessary. He was skilled at repairing the iron or the kitchen clock or figuring out why the heater didn't want to work or at tightening the clothesline. Then he'd sit down to read and listen to music. At family gatherings or in front of others, he was closemouthed and taciturn and didn't seem to be happy, but at home his presence could be felt. My brothers were scared of him. "Shhh, Pa's over there," they'd warn me.

He bought the house in Condesa, but we never had a car, and he traveled around the city by bus, never by taxi—no such luck—or he'd walk because he claimed he hadn't been born in a limousine.

He had his routine. Wednesday, every single Wednesday I can remember, he'd bring roses to my mother; now I imagine it was to ease his guilt. On Sunday he would take us downtown to buy sugar candies and crystallized fruit. We could keep half, because the other half, so he said, was for the agency secretaries. Or were they for his other family? And generally speaking, we'd have a coffee, milk and sweet roll breakfast in the Café Tacuba or in one of the Chinese restaurants on Dolores Street ("Good morning, *Mistel Leanlo, Sra. Dololes*," my brother Juan made fun). Then we'd walk around Alameda Park to Juárez y Madero Avenue or go down Cinco de Mayo until we reached the Zócalo, ending up for one o'clock Mass at Santo Domingo Church. Saturday was father's day off: he would go buy his used records or stop in the secondhand bookstores on Donceles Street or at the Tepito stands stocked with classics. His library was quite small, but very select: my brother Alberto inherited it. He loved to read biographies; his favorite, if I remember, was of Homer. He would reread the same books over and over. I bet that he knew whole paragraphs by heart.

My mother'd ask me: "Tell your father dinner's ready, to put his *Cármenes* down."

Or: "Tell him to put away *Las Tristes* and come cheer up his poor stomach."

When I turned fifteen, he gave me an old edition of *Daphne and Chloe.*

For years it was my favorite book and one, of course, that none of my classmates wanted to read. To me, it was a beautiful and wretched tale. Since reading it, I've had a fondness for unhappy endings.

My father would come home in his navy blue suit, take off the felt hat he always wore—as if still living in the forties— and put on the record player.

We liked very different music. He preferred opera (Alberto inherited his passion and his collection). My father also liked Baroque while my taste back then ran toward Romantic and Impressionist music.

"Corelli, like Bach, is precise."

"But I don't like precision," I'd shoot back.

"How can you not like Bach?" he'd ask angrily.

It's not that I didn't like him; after all, Bach is Bach. But I prefer playfulness, the Romantic gushes, the freedom.

My father was from the sticks, from another era: not only did he wear a hat, but suspenders, too, and he never wanted to buy a television. "To waste time? Is that why you want one?"

My brothers watched TV at their friends' houses and I secretly at the neighbor's after doing my homework. But I always felt like I was intruding, and I begged my mother to get him to change his mind. When I started seeing my stepbrothers more often and trusted them, I asked if they had a TV at home. When I found out they watched TV with my father, the conflicting feelings I had toward him flared up again. After what I've done, I couldn't cast the first stone at him.

Not owning a television is perhaps why I ended up listening to my father's records when he wasn't home. I'd put them on as I played with my dolls and pretend to go to a concert or I'd make believe I played the piano and they were my audience.

My father found this amusing, but still he would scold me, "Why can't you leave the records alone? You're so disorderly. I forbid you to play them. They cost a lot of money; you need to treat them with care."

But when I started at the National School of Music, he gave me the *Children's Corner* and *Claire de Lune*. It was silly of me to study at the conservatory and not have a piano. I knew we would never have a piano in the house. Never ever.

"I want a piano," I pleaded with my mother.

"Just that?"

"Well, also a TV..."

"You know your father."

You learn things so late. Back then we took father's reticence at home as his stubbornness, his whim, an absurdity we could not forgive. It was his way of underscoring his strictness.

When I was young, I remember asking him one night: "Did you have a grandma and grandpa?"

"I don't remember."

"Try."

"I can't."

"Why don't we ever see them?"

"They died."

"From what?"

"Go to bed."

"Try to remember."

It took pliers to get his parents' and grandparents' names out of him. Nothing else. But he lied when he claimed they had died when he was a kid. Our mother never elaborated on this.

I don't remember hearing my parents fight. Only once did I see my father lose control—when my brother Juan came home drunk from a party. It was a disaster for all of us, since he told Juan to take off his belt and he whipped him with it until my mother stepped in front of him. No one ever mentioned again what had happened that night.

When I told my father that I didn't want to go back to music school, he complained: "Do you think money grows on trees? I won't spend another penny on your education."

"I'm not a good pianist, everyone in the conservatory knows it. Why don't you ask the teachers? They'll tell you."

"That's a lie."

"Go ask them."

"You're lazy."

"I will never play the piano well, Dad. Understand?"

He didn't speak to me for a month and he kept his word: when I wanted to take dance classes, he wouldn't give me the money.

But mother put aside some of her spending money for my classes at the *Alliance Français* till I got a scholarship. But I never finished my course of study there, either. I'm not a good finisher. It's one of my shortcomings, a weakness, definitely a character trait.

We had fish soup, followed by white rice and San Lázaro style octopus in its ink. As we ate, I told my aunt and uncle about my brothers as if I ran into them every day. Of course, I didn't say that Alberto's wife is dumb, silly, frivolous, a mental case who has brainwashed my brother. I didn't tell them that Juan never got his degree and owns a car lot and was in jail for fraud. If it hadn't been for Rafael, who knows what would've happened. He got Juan out quickly, but Rafael was furious. I didn't tell them that just after my mother died, Alberto's wife phoned to ask me who would get the apartment, that she wanted my mother's furniture immediately because they had just finished renovating their house and wanted to put it in their daughter Susana's bedroom. These are the unspoken things that are embarrassing. I just told them generalities about my brothers and spoke of my mother as if she had no faults. As a child I had a pathological respect for her.

"Everyone at a given moment hates his parents," Rafael said to me one night, I don't remember why, as we talked before falling asleep.

"I didn't," I said.

"You don't want to admit it."

It wasn't a question of admitting anything. The most I could blame my mother for was for being so submissive, but that's the way women were back then.

Once, to help meet her expenses, she raised chickens on the terraced roof of our house. She sold eggs to the neighbors as if we were living in a village. The rooster was our alarm clock, the neighborhood alarm clock.

"Ask your mother if she'll sell me two eggs."

And I'd go into the kitchen to where Juan put the eggs every morning before he went off to school.

Suddenly my uncle excused himself. He went to take a nap in the hammock, and I stayed with my aunt looking at photographs. We could hear the hammock hoops creaking like a chronometer till he finally fell asleep.

I had expected something different. I had come full of hope, excited to meet my grandparents and uncles in photos, but as time passed and they didn't appear, I began to hate them. Curiosity and scorn, fantasy and disgust, desire and dislike struggled within me; but most of all, resentment triumphed inside me. And worst of all, my aunt showed me pictures I couldn't care about in the least.

"This is my son, Roque, at thirty."

Still, the photographs were somewhat interesting: they revealed an era, furniture, a way of dressing—what the people of San Lázaro were like.

There was no reason for me to stay any longer. Through the window I saw people going by, and I wanted to walk behind them, to free myself from this prison, this humiliating experience. My aunt traced her relatives and not her husband's and so I didn't see any photos of my grandparents or of the people that interested me.

I realized that my aunt and uncle had deceived me, that no matter how many pictures they showed me I would never see the ones they had promised. They wanted company and a bit of gossip and that made me furious. They had hurt me, intentionally or not.

Suddenly I stood up and glanced at my watch. "My husband will be calling me soon."

I grabbed my purse and left as my father and brothers

had done, cutting off the only possibility of communication, of having the family reunion I had longed for all my life.

I'll never think about those photographs again. What a stupid idea. What do I care what my grandparents were like, especially since they scorned my mother? "They must all have had ugly, sour faces," I wrote in my notebook that night.

"Just a maid," my uncle had said. I was born to a rich kid and a maid who as time passed was more dignified than her in-laws.

The rest of the afternoon I wandered though town to calm my nerves. What a big surprise! I shouldn't have expected anything different from the visit. I stopped at a crafts store and bought ships inside bottles for my sons and two cross-stitched embroidered blouses for myself. Then I wandered into an antique shop where I found some 19th century coins. One side said *The bearer worked for one cent* and the other *Ulumal Hacienda*. The second said *The bearer worked for 3 cents* with *Hacienda San Miguel* on the back. The third said *The bearer worked for 5 cents* and so on. I bought Rafael four coins, thinking that they made a nice gift.

"Today I worked as a laborer for just 5 cents in my uncle's house. Today I worked like a slave for just 3 cents in my uncle's house. Today I worked for 1 cent in my uncle's house. Today I worked for nothing in my uncle's house," I repeated like a prayer as I walked out of the shop.

My great-grandfather would've used those coins to pay the workers at his haciendas, and he would've liked to pay my mother a fistful of coins to forget my father.

I walked along the waterfront thinking of my father and Rafael. So different and yet so alike. I was thinking especially of Rafael. There are certain things you can't forget. Then I felt embarrassed remembering my betrayal...How sad the sun can suddenly become.

I finished writing down my dream. Then I realized I had nothing to do tomorrow since I had decided not to go back to the archives. I didn't need to get up early. I lit a cigarette and opened the curtains in my room. The sea was calm and the floating city barely moved. The streets of San Lázaro, empty now, looked infinitely more beautiful.

"What's wrong with me?" I thought. "What's happened to me these last few years?" I went to get a sleeping pill from my suitcase and found the box Eduardo had given me when we had met for lunch at the San Angel Inn. I took it out, got into bed and unfolded the sheets one by one as if I had just received them. Why am I like this? Why?

Chapter Eight

The chambermaid must have knocked several times, but not getting an answer, she opened the door. Perhaps she wanted to make up the room or make sure I was okay. I looked at my watch: 4 p.m. When at last I closed my eyes, almost at daybreak, I had fallen asleep like a rock. I vaguely remembered a dream in which Eduardo was driving my car and I was upset because he drove so badly. I had slept so deeply that I hadn't even heard the San Andrés bells. I asked the chambermaid to come back later and I called room service for breakfast or what was now a late lunch.

Pulling the curtains back, I saw a black sky signaling an impending storm.

I had an intense desire to hear music. "Men are like music," said Sra. Mari, the best teacher I ever had in school. "You think you know them without really knowing them. You have to decode them."

There were times I would listen to Satie as if I listening to Eduardo, with genuine curiosity. I enjoy trying to comprehend Satie's clarity, his transparency, until certain melodies begin to bore me. He can be so boring—*Ennuyez vous...non, ne jouez pas trop vite*—and yet his notes are amazingly pure. You can lose yourself in the beauty of Satie's music, in its depth, its playfulness, though sometimes his wit is as irritating, endless, tedious and painful as love: *Jouez vous...non, n'aimez pas trop vite. N'aimez pas trop vite.*

Had Eduardo fallen in love with me much too quickly? Was it my fault? What will happen next? Will he fall in love with someone else? Yes, I knew about what went on with his wife; he often discussed her with me and complained about his "woeful" home life.

Since this is a small world and life in big cities is insular, I met Ilona Soskay, Eduardo's wife, at an art opening of a friend of Rafael's. I hadn't known that she owned a Juan Manuel. When I found out who she was, I was full of hope, as if she could help me uncover another part of Eduardo. I didn't feel indignation, contempt or guilt. What would she have done had she known she was talking to her husband's lover? Had she ever suspected anything?

When Juan Manuel introduced me to her, my first reaction was to flee.

"Glad to meet you," I said, trying to walk away. But Juan Manuel wouldn't let me.

"Sra. Soskay collects Mexican art. This is Marcela Hernández. She's a designer, the best in the—"

"Don't believe him," I interrupted. "He says that because I designed the exhibit catalog."

"Congratulations. The catalog is very—"

"Do you collect Juan Manuel's art?" I interrupted.

There's a big difference in age between us, and she appeared much older than Eduardo. I looked at her as if examining a very old stamp with a magnifying glass. She wore a red wool tailored outfit with a silk kerchief around her throat, probably to hide the wrinkles. She was still beautiful, and I liked her fiery eyes, deepened by makeup and eye shadow. Her hair was light brown, almost blonde, and it seemed to glisten, to be full of life. Her smile didn't reveal a monster but rather a shrewd woman. "What's wrong with me?" I wondered. "How can I be so calm talking to this woman?" I had no desire to run or hide. After all, Ilona should be grateful to me for keeping her husband happy. And didn't Eduardo know Rafael?

Looking at her, I was aroused by the same curiosity that led me to explore where they lived in Mexico City and which one morning brought me to Cuernavaca, simply to drive by their house.

Ilona is interesting, she has her good points. When she married Eduardo in 1962, she took his last name and Mexican nationality without giving up—on her father's advice—her last name and her U.S. citizenship. According to Eduardo, she was born in California in 1938 and inherited the white skin, the tall and powerful body, the chestnut-colored hair and the facility for languages from her paternal great-grandfather. She speaks Spanish like a native and doesn't mix-up her genders or commit errors (like putting a feminine article on a masculine noun) commonly made by Americans.

Eduardo says that Ilona's great-grandmother spoke Hungarian, German and French—the principle languages of the Austro-Hungarian Empire. According to Ilona, her father Bernard Soskay told her that her grandmother spoke several other languages to the farmhands who brought wheat to her husband's mill or when she traveled through the Hapsburg empire.

Ilona's mother was an American of Scottish descent who met her husband in California. He was a young Hungarian who had arrived in New York in 1911 at age three. Ilona's grandfather—a nationalist who as a child had lived through Kossuth's revolution, which created the Hungarian Republic, later crushed by the Russians—raised horses. The best horses in her grandfather's stables went into the service of the Empire.

It seems that Ilona's grandfather was a man used to the countryside and farm animals, who couldn't adjust to life in America. He had just settled in Schenectady, New York when his wife died. He remarried, but within five years he was broke. He opened a tannery, but since he didn't speak English, he had a hard time making a go of the business.

The two oldest sons of Ilona's grandfather left the house to seek their fortunes and Bernard, her father, started working as a teenager so the children of his father's second marriage could go to college. At thirteen he apprenticed with General Electric in New York where he learned quite a bit about electricity and mechanics. But when he had the chance, he moved to California: he had always dreamed of having a farm, like his father. He got a job as a mail carrier, making deliveries in the San Fernando Valley. His last stop was Tarzana, a small town where Edgar Rice Burroughs was born and which was named after Tarzan. Ilona's grand-mother invited him for coffee one afternoon and, later, to a party where her cousin, an opera singer, was to sing passages from *La Boheme*. That's how her parents met.

Ilona wasn't raised on a farm but in the Albuquerque and Phoenix Indian reservations because Bernard Soskay started working, after the wedding, for a construction firm under contract to build schools and hospitals on the reservations. Ilona learned to read and write with Navaho children and graduated from elementary school with Hopi and Pueblo Indians.

Ilona's mother collected ceremonial jars, paintings and weavings which encouraged Ilona's passion for the arts while Bernard employed his mechanical and electrical skills to invent a molding machine to make concrete blocks. This machine was used by the Indians to make bricks for their homes. When he returned to California, he patented *The Soskay System* and then later started his own firm, *Concrete Products Mold Company*. Eduardo and Ilona had just married when Bernard Soskay tried to get him to introduce *The Soskay System* in Mexico, but Eduardo wasn't interested.

Ilona visited Mexico for the first time in 1955. She was a young 17 year old *gringa* when she came to spend a few days in the house of a couple she'd met in California, and who lived in Mexico City's Mixcoac district; a few days later she left their house never to return after the man threw himself on her.

Ilona left, suitcase in hand, to look for a cab, not sure

what she should do. She felt she was on a dark, uncertain path in an unknown country. She hailed a cab which took her to a pensión with a red-tiled roof and blue facade that she liked because of its balconies with geraniums.

Adolfo Ruiz Cortines was Mexico's president back then. If the landlady could be believed, a kilo of beans cost a peso and beef filet six. Since the exchange rate had been set at $12.50 pesos to the dollar the year before Ilona's trip, her savings (she had waited tables in the university cafeteria) had increased in value, allowing her to enjoy her first stay in Mexico free of money worries. Pensión Amalia was in Coyoacán, a village just outside Mexico City; she paid 15 pesos a day for a room and three meals. A pittance, a gift from Sra. Amalia, and the opportunity to experience authentic Mexican life.

Her room had a clay tile floor, an antique wardrobe, a brass bed, a yellow table and bench decorated with Mexican roses. From her window she could see volcanoes; back then Mexico City was in a transparent valley bathed in serenity, a landscape I never knew.

Ilona and I discussed Juan Manuel's painting.

"His colors reflect those of his nearby desert."

Ilona was not speaking metaphorically: Juan Manuel is from Zacatecas, and he doesn't deny his roots either in his paintings or ceramics. The browns, reds, and yellows of the Zacatecan desert are all there.

We drank white wine and Ilona told me how Sra. Amalia, a dark-skinned woman with white braids, had daintily placed the tortillas wrapped in a cotton napkin on the table and then proceeded to show her how to make tacos.

She not only discovered the tastes and variety of Mexican cooking at Sra. Amalia's pensión, but also learned about Talavera cuisine cooked over hot coals in the clay pots and casseroles which were hanging from the walls. Ilona also came down with typhoid, which they tried to cure with mint tea.

Sra. Amalia's oldest son, a mariachi singer in a Durango Street restaurant, had fallen in love with her. He never missed an opportunity to come with his guitar to the hallway and play Agustín Lara and Gonzalo Curiel boleros or José Alfredo Jiménez *rancheras* for her.

Back then Ilona was majoring in art at Berkeley. As a result of her studies, she knew Diego Rivera's work, and she went to look for him one day to interview him. He welcomed her to his San Angel studio, wearing a white robe and vest, the day before he was to leave for Moscow with his wife Emma Hurtado.

Ilona had bought carnations in the Mixcoac market and she gave them to his wife, telling him that she was studying art and wanted to interview him on behalf of her teacher. Rivera politely sent her away, telling her she could still change her field of study, but so she'd remember him and to thank her for the carnations she had brought his wife, he would give her a drawing. He took it out of his portfolio and so she acquired her first valuable art work. Ilona found out years later that he had given her a charcoal sketch on paper of Tina Modotti, a study for the 1926 painting now in the Philadelphia Museum of Art.

This is how Ilona fell in love with Mexico, its landscape and colors, its people and its music, its food and its markets. She knew she would return though her father distrusted Mexicans, claiming they had killed Maximillian, Emperor Franz Joseph's brother in 1867. And it wasn't that her father liked the Hapsburgs, but he thought it was inhuman to kill a deluded dreamer, a fool who believed it was more interesting to be Emperor of Mexico and sit on a fictitious throne than to be an Austrian archduke and go hunting on horseback.

Ilona told me that night that she had gone to Chapultepec Castle to photograph both Maximillian's carriage and the saddle he rode when he was captured. She sent the pictures to her father with the note:

Are Maximillian's horses the brothers of those Grandfather Istvan raised for Franz Joseph?

Soskay's family gave him no title when they referred to the last Hapsburg who subdued the Hungarians.

Eduardo met Ilona in 1960. She had returned to Mexico and worked in the U.S. Cultural Relations Institute on Hamburgo Street where he was studying English. They got married two years later, after Eduardo returned from Stanford as a specialist in cardiology and had landed a job and a decent salary.

A bright-eyed American with an art degree who was in love with Mexico and listened to Agustín Lara and swore, as if she were an expert or it was in her blood, that Arruza was courageous. She shared an apartment with other Americans on Río Duero Street, facing Melchor Ocampo Park. A plump girl with chestnut-colored hair and round, green eyes.

Back then they both were sure of themselves and confident. There were weekends in Cuernavaca, where he recovered from the stress of hospital work and she— encouraged by her countryman Robert Brady, an eccentric, gay art collector living in Cuernavaca who introduced her to actresses and painters alike—searched with saintly patience for an old house to renovate or bought antiques or one-of-a-kind pieces from the different artisans living in the villages surrounding Cuernavaca. Peace reigned in the apartment they had purchased in Mexico City's *Condesa* building. They'd have friends over or would stay home to read, listen to music, do nothing. Eduardo looked upon Soskay with the interest one feels for another person's life because there are secrets yet to be revealed and they seemed a fabulous couple like all new couples who've just had a child who will study abroad, marry a Frenchman, and live in Italy.

Ilona's trips to Mexican villages kept her appreciation of Mexican culture alive and also helped her develop a collection of textiles, *Talavera* and *La Granja* ceramics, gold-painted glass, *pulque* jars, wrought iron—objects that were mostly from the colonial period. The collection grew without Eduardo realizing how valuable it had become, like the rebozo collection Ilona now owned. This was the first thing Ilona spoke to me about at Juan Manuel's show, when she saw me in my mother's rebozo. She went on to tell me that that kind of weaving was no longer done—it must be nearly a hundred years old, an authentic Santa María shawl. I should take good care of it or she would gladly buy it from me. Then I realized it must have belonged to my grandmother. I may be wrong, but Ilona's textiles are comparable to those of the Belgian Robert Evert in the Franz Mayer Museum.

"I hate her" were the words Eduardo spurted one morning, for no reason, as he was about to shave at the mirror. "I detest her," he said sadly, knowing that only far from her could he avoid such a contemptible feeling. Only by distancing himself could he recall the rosy fleshed Ilona Soskay of his youth, but now he lacked the courage to divorce her.

They aged at the same time, but Eduardo suspects that something in Ilona's life placed an ugly expression on a face that had once been fresh and seductive. Yet Ilona's face is still beautiful despite the years and I didn't perceive any traces of ugliness in her wrinkles.

Eduardo insists that he tried to make Ilona happy, but then realized that no one can decree the happiness of another. He was tired, disheartened, exhausted from trying. How was he to know they would end up like this? How could he imagine that his marriage would turn into polite resignation, in a distancing that became more and more disagreeable even if he continued to act differently from what he felt? Hadn't he sworn fidelity to the Ilona still loved in the memory of those first years of marriage, she who had been natural, anything but solemn, with a good sense of humor and most of all with encouragement and joy for his accomplishments? But the Ilona of recent memory was not only upset by his successes but also by his friendships. Or at the very least, that's what he assured me, but I don't know if it's true.

For some time he controlled his frame of mind to bear the situation, to the point that Ilona wouldn't have known if he were tired, depressed, angry or in love. He played his role so well in this comedy that fiction became fact. I think that if Eduardo had been able to extend those first years of marriage, without thinking that one day he would succeed through patience or fail through bitterness, he would have prolonged those years even if he were unsure which of the two would be in his future.

That night, at Juan Manuel's opening, I compared myself to Eduardo's wife: What did I have over her other than youth? No, I am not trying to underrate myself. Although I have two growing boys, a career I enjoy, and have tasted a bit of everything, perhaps my sense of personal satisfaction is insignificant compared to Ilona's, or so I thought. Still, Ilona might have been envious of the many things I can do—like change my habits and my life—and I don't think she could start anew separated from Eduardo. And whereas she had lost all interest in him, I flattered him, commented on his clothes, his haircut, his food, his pleasures and problems. I shared his professional successes, his readings and his passion for music, and I amused myself admiring and seducing him and pleasing him as if he were a child, making him feel attractive, charming, intelligent and manly. She not only didn't care about this, she was actually a shadow, a weight, a bother, the constant reminder of a perverted and lost world and of a relationship he had to bear and put aside as soon as possible.

Looking at Ilona, I thought: "You"—how could I speak to her and not use the formal case—"can believe we have nothing more in common than Juan Manuel or his work. You don't know we share more than that: we have caressed the same hair, kissed the same mouth. We both have made Eduardo feel loved; feeling loved makes one serene, confident, satisfied and pleased. But you, Ilona, have lost interest in him while I'd give anything to live at his side."

I wasn't scared but also didn't want to act as if nothing was happening. My enemy was before me and I didn't want to lose the chance to compare myself to her and know that even with nothing but age in my favor, I could triumph over her because my love wasn't a passing fancy. My mind also wandered into worse places: How good was Ilona in bed? And I remembered his words:

Even making love to my wife at night was easier. Does it hurt for me to tell you this?

This implied that their relations were not good.

"Your husband," I finally said, "cared for my mother. He's an interesting man; I admire and respect him."

"He works too much," she replied.

"But he's charming," I insisted.

"That's what his patients say," she clarified.

"He's a very gentle man, very..."

"He had a good teacher," she cut me off.

When someone talks to me about Rafael, praising his work or his personality, I go on to say—because I believe it—that he is one of Mexico's best lawyers and a brilliant man. Ilona obviously did not recognize Eduardo's talents.

"How long have you been living in Mexico?" I asked, changing the subject.

Ilona was once more charming and spoke with great energy and joy, almost bubbly; it was hard for me to believe Eduardo's version of his martyrdom and suffering.

The storm broke sooner than I expected. How it rains in the tropics! I felt like crawling back into bed. I was so tired. After eating, I'd fall back asleep. "What's wrong with me?" I wondered. "Am I going to stay locked in here?"

I'd have gone out during the storm if I could have run into Eduardo. At times I felt that if I couldn't be with him I would die. But the last time we were together, I noticed that he didn't want to look me in the eyes. And as if it were a huge effort, he said: "I'm not going to see you again."

I didn't answer him, only thought: "I'm going to die of sadness."

It was strange being with him, knowing I would never again caress him and that quite possibly Eduardo despised me like he hated his wife (if it's true) that morning he looked at himself in the mirror.

I glanced at my bed. I'm going back to sleep. I won't eat, just get back into bed. I'll sleep until the storm is over. When you want nothing from life but to sleep and you hide your watch so you won't see the time and you don't even care what day it is and there's nothing you can do to avoid sleep, it's like dying. And that's how I felt because I had to decide what to do with my life without Eduardo and if I were going to separate from Rafael.

Chapter Nine

The storm passed through faster than expected. My food was brought up, and the chambermaid came back to make my bed and clean the room. While she worked, I ate the snapper stew and the stewed plums I had ordered. I felt accompanied and grateful to have someone moving around the room, demonstrating confidence in her cleaning skills even if we exchanged no words. She was a short, stocky and powerful woman who lifted the mattress as if it were a banana leaf or a goose feather. When she bent down to mop under the bed, I saw the varicose veins on her legs and thought she was much too young to have them. I wanted to ask if they were painful, if she had seen a doctor, but I didn't have the courage.

When she caught me looking at her, she said: "Aren't you going out? The weather's improved. That's what it's like this time of year: the sky turns black, the rain falls, it cools down for a while and the heat returns, that's it. We need more rain for the fields, but the water is so stingy. Only hurricanes don't deceive the land, but see, they destroy everything."

I didn't answer her, but through the mirror I saw a hint of a smile on her face.

"That's how storms are," I mumbled. "But storms end, don't they?"

I wasn't in the mood to chat—the people from San Lázaro are cheerful and talkative and if you give them half a chance, they go on and on. I wanted her to finish quickly so I could go back to my letters.

When she finally left, I took a long bath in warm water. Later, with a towel wrapped around my body, I paced back and forth in the room trying to clear my mind of everything. I didn't want to think, but I kept repeating obsessively: "That's what storms are like. Just like that. That's what storms are like."

Suddenly the song I hadn't heard for a while started up again. "Oh no," I thought, "not again. What a nightmare." And yet I liked the lyrics:

> There was a boy
> a very strange and enchanted boy,
> they say he wandered very far,
> very far, over land and sea...

I imagined that the couple had returned from some trip to the outskirts of San Lázaro. There are so many colonial towns nearby: if they lack a pyramid, a convent or a church, they at least have the ruins of a 19th century hacienda. Shouldn't I at least go visit what had been my great-grandfather's haciendas? Would anything be left standing?

I opened the door to the balcony to watch the sun going down. That door was my connection to the world. When it was closed, every part of me was in turmoil. I looked toward the balcony next door and saw several items of clothes drying on the terrace chairs. The rain must have caught them by surprise and now they were getting ready to go out again. "If they keep playing that damn ballad," I said to myself, "I'm going to complain to the management."

The sky was blue once more. The chambermaid had been right: the air was thin and easy to breathe, but a few city streets were flooded and people walked along sidestepping the puddles.

I decided to call Rafael and then sit on the terrace to read Eduardo's letters. To be able to read them freely, to reread them and ponder over the words, to memorize and then forget them was one of the reasons for this trip. Somehow I wasn't really up for it—I'd read them in spurts or I'd drink too much so as to lose them in a corner of my subconscious or I'd make up any excuse to put off dealing with them because maybe I knew that nothing could be salvaged from our affair.

I called Rafael's office and then our house, but he wasn't at either place.

I didn't want to think about Rafael or our relationship again. I had done that so many nights, coming up with a different solution each time, that I was more confused than I had expected. One day I wanted to separate, the next divorce, the third to confess everything, but most often, to throw myself into his arms and cry. One night I decided I didn't love him, the next that I had never stopped loving him, and the third, that it was all his fault. That often happens: I tend to blame others for my own mistakes.

I thought about my children. How would they accept a separation or how would a divorce affect them? What would they say? Would they understand that when you fall in love you take leave of your senses? No way. They were almost teenagers, and teenagers view the world as being more complex than it actually is. I was afraid of their response or perhaps their shock or confusion.

It wasn't as if I planned to run off with Eduardo, that wasn't the solution. What I couldn't do was live with Rafael as if nothing had happened, as I had been doing up till now. At first, when I began going out more steadily with Eduardo, I was even happier with my husband. Later, I'd give anything to get out of the house, and then…I was at the crossroads between repentance and doubt.

I had met Rafael just after turning seventeen. I was in high school and felt a confusion as profound as the one now paralyzing me in San Lázaro. It's as if I've always lived in utter confusion. Well, yes. It's how I am; it's my fate, my blinking star that's startled by everything that befalls me.

Back then the issue was my father's recent death, and life around the house had become more somber; I say more because it had never been joyful. I had and still have a calm temperament. My life was peaceful and unchanging, somber and boring.

At seventeen, I'd give anything to go to the movies, to a café or to waste time like my classmates who spent the whole afternoon talking on the phone or watching TV. But getting my mother's permission was too difficult and though we had a TV, she was the one glued to it. She would pass the time watching soaps while darning my brothers' socks or knitting infant blouses, that later she sold to a baby shop on Zamora Street. She'd sigh every so often because she was alone and couldn't control my brothers because, according to her, they did whatever they damn well pleased.

My only true distraction was reading or listening to music. I rummaged through my father's books: *Samuel Pepys's Diary*, or biographies such as *Richard V, Lucretia Borgia, Queen Victoria, The Life of Sara Bernhardt, Napoleon II, Catherine the Great...*

I would read while listening to my brothers' records. Alberto liked Gershwin (*An American in Paris* was his favorite), the Doors, the Rolling Stones (*Start Me Up*). Juan went crazy over Bernstein's *West Side Story*, Blood, Sweat & Tears's *Spinning Wheel* and *You've Made Me So Very Happy* and The Beatles's *From Me to You* and *All You Need Is Love*. Of my father's records, I preferred back then those by popular groups, romantic trios such as *Los Tres Ases* and *Los Panchos*. The classical pieces I liked were Chopin's *Nocturnes* and Schumann's *Songs for an Early Hour*.

I missed my piano classes, mostly because I had lost my independence; you see, now I took a cab three times a week to the *Alliance Française*, but the rest of the time I had no escape from the monotony of my limited world. I stayed in, after doing my homework, helping my mother iron or clean the fridge or the pantry or my brothers' closet.

"What are you doing?" she'd shout.

"Reading."

"Come give me a hand, then," she'd order, as if reading were a waste of time.

I'd give anything to get out of the house, to go anywhere. I wished my mother would die, horrible as it sounds, to have no family, to live alone and be able to come and go as I pleased. I wanted to go anywhere, study anything besides French after school, whether it was typing, shorthand, ceramics, or painting. Actually, I'd never had the discipline to study seriously. I only wanted to sample, as my father said; if it had been up to me, I'd have spent my whole life sampling.

I met Rafael at the birthday party of Sofía, my classmate at the Madox Academy. He seemed more serious than handsome. Rafael is tall, thin, dark-skinned with huge, lively eyes, but not good-looking. He has his fine points: when he laughs, his open and honest smile is appealing and contrasts with his seriousness. I was seduced by his confidence, because he oozes self-assurance, and by his readiness to argue, debate and analyze. He has a fighting, combative spirit. And he's decisive.

That night he didn't even look at me, stayed barely a few minutes. Weeks later I asked Sofía about him. She said he studied law and worked in his father's office.

"You like him, eh?"

In those days I was attracted to all young men, but as soon as they came near me, I lost interest. I had liked it that Rafael had not strutted about.

I saw him some time later. He was at Sofía's house one Saturday when I went over to study with her. He was twenty-three then, about to get his degree.

His family had come to Mexico City from Chiapas. They were wealthy; his grandfather had coffee plantations in Tapachula and though his mother had her teaching certificate, she didn't work. Rafael's father had a law office,

Hernández, Serrano and Associates. They handled civil, commercial and criminal cases primarily for clients from Chiapas, and were quite successful. That's why Rafael owned a car, studied at a private university and was thinking of going to the U.S. for post-grad work, which he eventually did.

Rafael's house had a swimming pool, a jai-alai court and on weekends, Sofía gossiped, there was always a party.

"Next time he invites me, I'll bring you along so you can see his fabulous house."

She brought me and I fell in love with him, his energy, his self-sufficiency, his belligerence, his lawyerly ways.

While doing his postgraduate work, Rafael sent me a postcard to Sofía's house: *I hope you remember me. Rafael.*

He never wrote me a letter, and if he had, it would've read like a contract; but when he returned two years later, he called and invited me for ice-cream. We went to Chiandoni, close to my house, and we started dating. We didn't get married when I finished studying design—not easy but I liked it because I had a lot of leeway and didn't have to kill myself studying—but when I was pregnant with Rafaelito. I hadn't been careful. "If I have a girl," I thought, "as soon as she has her first period, I'm going to give her my grandmother's earrings and a box of contraceptives." I was dying to get out of the house and we were wildly passionate—we were quite young. My mother threw a fit, my brothers reacted badly, but Rafael took it all in stride.

Since my mother had no money, Rafael's father covered the wedding. Like a good lawyer, he argued that he had lots of obligations and a big family. And yes, I think half of Chiapas came to the wedding.

When my father-in-law retired, Rafael took over the business, the client list, and worked around the clock. We lived in a tiny apartment in the Del Valle district while our new house in Las Aguilas was being built. I had my second son and when the two of them began elementary school, I looked for work. I got a job in an ad agency; it was like a breath of fresh air because I despaired of staying alone in the house while Rafael was conspicuous by his absence.

Rafael was a different kind of husband, not what I had expected, because he shared few things with me and our children. Perhaps because my father—with his passivity, his solitary and taciturn nature—was my model, I liked Rafael's being out of the house. But whenever I asked him not to go back to work after lunch or to take me to the movies or mentioned that we needed this or that or for him to repair something, he'd argue that he had no time because he was working on a very delicate and very, very, very difficult case. And he'd take care of everything by sending me his chauffeur who is as skilled with a hammer, a screwdriver, and pliers as with a pick and shovel, or a shopping list, or serving lunch or mixing drinks.

"I should've married Pancho," I told him one night, "I spend more time with him than with you. I hate your clients. I hate your partners. I hate all your delicate and consuming cases, your courthouses, and your juries!"

Rafael laughed as if I were joking, but it was a complaint he just didn't get.

Like his father, and I suppose his grandfather too, he loves company. He simply calls and says: "The Gonzálezes are coming for dinner. I'll send Pancho to help you."

I don't mind the dinners. What I don't like is sharing with others the little time I have with Rafael.

It was different with Eduardo: a delicate and cautious relationship, unhurried. Everything about him surprised me—his politeness, his sensitivity, not what one would expect from a doctor. He not only appreciated painting but music too, and this allowed us to develop another kind of communication. He was solicitous and would cancel appointments so we could be together.

At the start, I actually saw very little of him. Every once in a while he would call and we saw each other perhaps every two or three weeks. We'd go to lunch or meet for breakfast or a coffee or go to a museum or a gallery. We'd make a date to meet somewhere like a Sanborn's or a Vips, or at the Perisur or Plaza Inn mall. I'd leave my car in the parking lot and join him and he would drive his car slowly, more attentive to the conversation than to the traffic. Little by little I realized that Eduardo's vision was deteriorating and that he was an inept, not to say downright bad, driver. He'd drive into the same potholes over and over and couldn't read the street names. I was very patient, didn't say anything, not a word about going through a stop sign or not being able to find the street we were looking for...He'd forget his glasses and have me read the menu or the title of a painting to him. I wanted neither to embarrass him nor make him feel old.

We were both burning with desire but nothing happened. He didn't rush me and I didn't force myself on him. We kept our distance and became more intimate through our letters. We did very simple things. I know that if I had confided in anyone, that person would've said "he's probably gay." But that's how we wanted it, with our correspondence being the most passionate aspect. An old-fashioned, somewhat 19th century type of relationship, harking back to my grandparent's era, perhaps.

Moreover, for Eduardo it was a kind of exercise, a warm-up for his letters:

...These letters are an opportunity and a diversion, Marcela, a way to answer to myself certain questions that I had never posed or had the time to deal with: to be able to reflect upon my passage through this world and my attitude toward my contemporaries, although no one is so perverse or innocent as to speak the truth about his own life. Marcela, maybe one day I'll revise these letters or what they led to and publish them if there's something worthwhile in them. I always wanted to write a novel, even if its publication would confirm the worst of what my enemies say about me.

I ask myself so many questions. Would he divulge his love affairs? Would he rationalize away what we, the women who have loved him, would say about him? Would he tell them what he told me? Had they felt what I now feel?

I haven't thought of anything but you, Marcela. It's rare to run into a woman and feel such need to be with her. Let me love you, let me tell you, Marcela, what's in my heart...

Why through letters? Before going on, I must confess that Eduardo has not asked for them back. It's strange: he must regret having said so many things because he always expressed himself freely, revealing his true nature or how he ultimately wanted to see himself. And he was even a bit melodramatic: "Let me tell you, Marcela, what's in my heart." Who wouldn't want to erase one's mistakes and failures?

It was the kind of relationship that bound us to one another, but also lessened the guilt and helped us maintain and continue the love affair. It was a loving friendship, corny and foolish, but passionate. Life-giving.

More than anything, I wanted to lose myself in the power of a woman to interpret—with humanity, delicacy and knowledge—from deep inside her a work of art so difficult to understand.

That's what I think of you, Marcela. That's how I want a woman with me, capable of interpreting in her intimacy my desire for tenderness. At my age tenderness is vital—ridiculous as it may sound, absurd as my saying it must seem.

He was referring to Mozart's sonatas. Uchida is my favorite Mozart interpreter. I've never seen her perform, but I've read reviews in which the audience doesn't like her because she overdramatizes her piano-playing. I'd forgive all the bravado because she plays like an angel, with the grace of God. I neither need nor want to see her, it's enough to hear her.

I tried calling Rafael again with no luck. No one knew when he would be returning to the office. I had forgotten, for a change, to call him last night. I know it wasn't exactly forgetfulness, but a desire not to face him.

The song played over and over next door.

> The greatest thing
> you'll ever learn
> is to love and be loved
> in return.

I put my clothes on and went next door to put an end to the music, once and for all.

Chapter Ten

"Who is it?" a hesitant voice asked in English.

"Your neighbor," I replied.

The young man with the buzz-cut finally appeared, in shorts and shirtless, revealing his strong, muscular chest. He was barefoot and rubbed his left foot with his right as he eyed me impatiently. The room reeked of burning straw.

"Turn off the music or lower it. Otherwise, I'll complain to the management," I said, going back to room 328, my refuge.

He slammed the door, but I didn't hear another sound.

I threw myself down on the bed with Eduardo's letters. I was putting them in chronological order, to read them as I had received them, when the phone rang. I thought it might be Rafael.

"Marcela?" a woman said.

"Speaking."

"Girl, it was difficult to find you. You told me you were staying here, but not that your last name was Hernández. I'm in the lobby."

"Who are you?"

"María Canto, the director of the archives."

"What's up?"

"I have a surprise for you. We've been expecting your visit."

"Something came up," I replied. I didn't want to tell her that I didn't want anything to do with my grandfather and his family.

"Can you come down?"

"Do I owe you something?"

"I didn't come to charge you."

"Give me ten minutes."

"We'll be at the bar."

"Who's with you?"

"Miguel."

"Miguel who?"

"We'll be at the bar," she repeated.

Encouraged by Sra. Canto's friendly voice, I put on a new pair of slacks and blouse, brushed my hair, put on makeup; I put Eduardo's letters back in my suitcase as if this is what I wanted to do with them. I locked the suitcase and threw the key in my purse. It seemed that I would never read them start to finish. Why was I so afraid? I considered staying in my room, not going downstairs.

Miguel was middle-aged, dark, with few gray hairs; he had lively black eyes and a sturdy build. But what an ugly man! I don't know if it was his thick eyebrows, his hawk-like nose or his long face that made him so unattractive. He was laughing his head off when I approached them.

"What are you laughing about?"

"Hi, this is Miguel."

"Your husband?"

"She refused me," he said mockingly.

I ordered a tequila, waiting for either of them to let out the surprise.

"What have you been up to?" Sra. Canto asked.

"Walking around San Lázaro."

But I hadn't walked anywhere, just acknowledged what was mine. During my walk I recovered what my grandparents had stolen before I had been born. They had concealed the memory of San Lázaro: the character of the people, the roguish women, the cheerfulness of its old folks, the bright clothing, the blue sky, the turquoise sea, the humidity, the salt-eaten walls, the fish smell of the kitchens, the tropical music blaring from house radios, the rocking chairs right on the sidewalk where the women enjoyed the breeze and talked about their children and grandchildren, the Indian stares, the accent of the people in the market, the smell of the almond trees....I had been stripped of it all by my grandparents and that afternoon I had suddenly gotten it all back.

"Around San Lázaro?" Miguel asked.

"Well, in the downtown area, the historical district..."

"I'm going to show you San Lázaro," he declared authoritatively, which didn't make a good impression on me.

Yet somehow I felt happy to be in their company although I didn't know them. Honest, happy, easygoing people...Since coming to town, I had had a sustained conversation only with my Souza relatives. I hadn't realized how much I needed to speak to someone, to be with friendly people.

I told them about my visit to the Souzas and the sudden contempt that I felt for my father's family. I admitted that I wasn't planning to return to the archives, and if they hadn't sought me out at the hotel, I wouldn't have seen them. "It seems you'll be followed to Mexico City by some papers you never picked up in San Lázaro," I thought. But the people here, I supposed, were like that, using any excuse just to pay a social call. But they had other reasons for their visit.

Miguel and Sra. Canto, like typical natives of San Lázaro, laughed a lot and made jokes. He brought me certificates of baptism, marriage and death for my relatives and a few notes as well. He had put it all in a yellow folder he kept on the stool next to him and tapped every so often.

"What do you do?" I asked him.

"I'm a historian. I teach at San Lázaro's Autonomous University."

"I don't believe you." He had a shopkeeper's face from the Lagunilla or La Merced flea market, the face of a rich Arab or hotel owner.

"I'm writing a book on the migrations to San Lázaro,

the mixing and breeding of people, so to speak. My project also studies the increased diversification of the economy. María and I have been friends for a long time. Sometimes, I stick my nose into the Archbishop's Archives. The certificates I find there play an important role in my research."

"But did you or someone else find mine? I don't get it."

"The Souzas are part of my research; besides, they've been friends of the family for generations. A while ago I went through the archives and copied a few certificates which I've brought along with me."

"Why did they interest you?"

"They're an atypical family of that period. I don't know if you know what I know."

"What do you mean?"

"Look here," he said, handing me the yellow folder.

I gave it back. "I prefer not to know."

It's not easy to accept that your grandparents snubbed your mother. It was something that hurt me even if I wasn't ready to accept it.

"Know nothing?"

"I made a mistake or, if you prefer, I regret having searched it out. I don't want to know anything."

"Okay, but listen to me. I'm also interested in you, as part of the family. That's why I came; I asked María to introduce us. She happened to mention that you had been to the Archives."

"Well, I have nothing to do with the family here. When my father left, he cut his cord. Poof!" I pretended my fingers were scissors cutting something. "He never said a thing about his family. They must've been a pile of shit, like my uncles."

"You don't beat around the bush, do you?" asked María.

"You should at least know the sociological facts regarding your family. They're worth knowing."

"How boring!"

"Stubborn, aren't you?"

"Sociological facts? What's that? Who cares? We'd better have another drink," I proposed.

"Another round," Miguel said to the bartender and went on: "The Souzas have lived in San Andrés, in the so-called *chic* neighborhood, since the Spanish conquest. Where those with economic and political power lived, the ones who made money. The certificates make clear their social and economic position."

"Miguel, you don't need a certificate to know that if they lived downtown they were rich. You only need to see their houses—to build and maintain them must've cost a fortune."

Sra. Canto seemed amused by our discussion.

"Pigheaded," Miguel said to me, glancing back at her.

"I'm right." I was getting ticked off, he seemed such a rustic historian.

"Still you should read the certificates, even if it's for sheer pleasure. The writing is amusing and says a lot. It's poetic: 'The exorcisms, oils, chrisms, and other baptismal rites were carried out in the Holy Parish of...' For the baptisms of the mestizos, the Indians and those with mixed blood living in other neighborhoods it simply states 'he solemnly received his Holy Baptism in such and such Holy Church.'"

"The rich were exorcised and the poor weren't? Is that what you want me to know? There's nothing new in claiming that the Church was also racist."

"You're right," he admitted. "Same thing happened with the burials: 'I buried so and so with a high cross, chalice, processional candlesticks, and six witnesses: three dressed in dalmatic vestments and three in surplices. Full wake, tomb and chapel, half a chorus properly attired, and a sung Mass...' It's like reading a novel. The rich had a complete and full ceremonial burial."

Sra. Canto broke in: "The certificates of those living on

the outskirts were different. They say, Doña Dolores Canto died of heart trouble in the San Martín district at age sixty-nine, having received the eucharistic penitence and extreme unction sacraments. The funereal rites were carried out in the church of the corresponding neighborhood..."

"Huh!" I answered, a bit tipsy.

I was bored and downed the last drops of tequila.

"You really don't want to know what your grandparents died of, who were the godparents at the baptisms, how old they were when they married, who their parents were? Things like that, which help make biographies," Miguel asked.

"I prefer another tequila and to change the subject."

"Okay, but I want to give you one more fact to arouse your curiosity."

"I already told you—"

He interrupted me. "Like others, the Souzas married people from other districts, but I tracked down marriages to Indians and blacks. That was rare; that's why I said your family was atypical for the period. To marry out of your area meant you jeopardized both your wealth and social ranking. There's a marriage to a black woman from Santa Ana. Very unusual. She was a slave. And later, someone married a San Martín Indian; he may have been a descendant of the pre-Colombian nobility, but still he was an Indian."

Ugly as he was, Miguel was attractive and manly. His eyes, his intensity, swept me up or else I was completely drunk. He'd toss back with his hand a cowlick that fell across his forehead, reminding me of Eduardo who did the same time when he had drunk too much.

"I have Jewish, Black, Indian, and a cook's blood," I dramatized to Sra. Canto.

"All of it shows, except the cooking part," she laughed.

"What do you want to do?" I said, looking at Sra. Canto

and changing the subject. "Let me take you both out to dinner. To a good restaurant. You choose it."

"Thank you, but I can't," Sra. Canto said.

Miguel, on the other hand, looked at me and said: "I'd love to take you around San Lázaro and then to El Bucanero. But it's on me."

"But whom do I pay for the copies and transcriptions?"

"Forget it," Miguel answered. "Don't insult us. Another drink and off we go."

I felt comfortable, happy, distracted. As if they were lifelong friends.

Miguel handed me the folder. "I don't want to carry this around. Drop it off at the front desk when we leave; it's up to you if you want to read it later."

Chapter Eleven

Miguel had a convertible sports car, but since the weather was bad, we left the top up and went to drop off María Canto near Carey Street, in the Santa Inés neighborhood, which is well-known for its music. We could hear cornets, trombones, tubas, trumpets, and drums and cymbals coming from the bandstand in the middle of the square; when the band wasn't playing, it was strange to hear crickets chirping, stirred up by the storm. The people circled the square, as they had for years: women walking clockwise and the unmarried men counterclockwise, watching them.

Sra. Canto invited us in for a drink, but Miguel told her: "What? You want me to lose the chance to abduct this woman? No way."

At the moment I actually preferred her invitation to walking around the Santa Inés Plaza or driving through San Lázaro, but I was ready to go anywhere. I wanted companionship and conversation: anything would be fine as long as it put off having to face the truth.

Miguel took me to the farthest city ramparts on the San Marcos hill. We were too late to catch the sunset; it was already night and too late to walk through the small museum which, according to my guidebook, displayed pre-Hispanic artifacts, muskets, cannons used against the pirates and navigational instruments. I was grateful that Miguel wasn't tossing off historical tidbits or treating me like a tourist to whom he could show off. We enjoyed gazing out to sea, barely illuminated by the lighthouse, the sailing ships and the city down below, which reminded me of Justine's

Alexandria. We were silent, walking calmly along the inside of the ramparts. Leaning against a parapet, I looked out at the sky flush with stars until Miguel brought me back to earth. "You can take it with you so you won't miss it so much."

He was playful, but more than that, trustworthy. He told me he had divorced years ago, had two daughters, and enjoyed the bachelor life and his university classes.

He took me from the San Marcos hill to the exclusive San Lázaro district, which circles the city from above and where huge mansions looked out over the sea. Private neighborhoods with pretentious names such as Seabreeze, Bellavista, Oceanview. We then drove through a different part of San Lázaro, lit up by a moonlight I hadn't expected, where the poverty surprised me. The contrast between the rich and the poor was stark. We went through a series of neighborhoods, without electricity or plumbing, which no tourist would ever see. Since it had rained so hard, the dirt roads were flooded and some streets completely impassable.

The genuine San Lázaro is hidden behind the hills surrounding the walled-in city. That's where the people with other faces, other looks, other ways of dressing and walking live, infused with the odor of corn and sweat. These are the people who come from the interior looking for work. The puddles and the heat gave a rotten and decomposing stench to the streets—this was a marsh, a quagmire, a swamp.

"This is the 'Sunrise' district."

"Hmm."

"That one over there is 'Conciliation.'"

I couldn't speak.

"This one is 'Stopover.'"

Though they had different names, they were the same: crowded shacks—full of children screaming—piled on top of one another on calcified hills, built of rotten wood, on the edge of sloping narrow paths, with bony dogs roaming. Where were the carpets of grassland, the palm trees, the avocado, the mango, the almond trees? The *quebracho* trees you could see on the farms, the haciendas, the mansions of the wealthy communities we had just driven through?

"Let's get out of here," I begged.

"It's like with your family. You don't want to see who they were. You're afraid."

"It's a crime."

"Are you scared to see your own people?"

"My grandfather must've been a sour old man; and if you want to know the truth, I hate my father—"

Even today I still can't understand how he could have had two families at the same time. How could he live a double life and not lose sleep? Wasn't I repeating the pattern? Hadn't I learned it from him? Honestly, I don't understand it. What did he do when one of his other children got sick?

After my mother died, I met his other wife. Rafael and I ran into one of my stepbrothers at Sanborn's one evening and he introduced her to us. Younger than my mother, but not more distinguished or beautiful. I felt pity, not anger, toward her. She must have been alone most of the time—without my father. Breakfast, lunch and dinner alone, alone to care for the children, alone to face her problems. Alone day and night, except for Saturdays.

"Every family has a skeleton in the closet," Miguel said, holding my hand in solidarity.

"But—"

"If you also 'want me to tell you,' your family was among the most hated in the region. Your great-grandfather was despised not so much for being an exploiter as for being a scoundrel, a filthy *cacique*. Almost all the Souzas set about to make money, to do their dirty deals. All kinds of business from selling Indians into slavery in Cuba to buying off people in the government to avoid sales and income taxes. The Souza who married the black woman from Santa Ana was disinherited, as your father was, and died drunk; and the woman who married the San Martín Indian was found hanging in a warehouse, evidently a suicide. Facing reality is important every now and again. Reality is nothing more than what it is. You have to go on living."

I didn't know what to say.

"The best thing your father did was leave this place; and more power to him if he gave himself the luxury of living."

"At the price of my mother's happiness?"

"You don't know if your mother wanted to live."

Even now, when I remember my parents, I'm not sure if Miguel wasn't right.

"I've now told you part of what you didn't want to hear. You can either forget it or not. No family gets away free."

"Not even yours?"

"Starting with me—I abandoned my daughters. I'm not on speaking terms with my brothers over my father's inheritance…"

That wasn't a new subject to me. Hadn't my sister-in-law claimed my mother's furnishings? Didn't Alberto's wife ask me for my mother's little sapphire? My son Felipe used to say that the ring must've come from a box of cereal, but even so, my sister-in-law had remembered it.

"Your mother didn't remember her other grand-children, just your boys," Miguel criticized, as if my mother had to leave something to people who neither cared for her nor visited her when she was sick. She left her apartment to my children.

Neither of us said anything. Then Miguel, changing his tone, said; "I asked you out so you'd have some fun."

I remained silent, not out of annoyance. Miguel was a person of unquestionable precision. I liked his style. His car carefully climbed the slopes and went across puddles slowly as if inattention could turn his car into a boat. From the San Carlos hill we could see the lights of the city once more and those of the ships in the small bay far off. I could have stayed there all night, looking at the view.

"I didn't know there were two San Lázaros," I said, breaking the silence.

"We conceal what we don't like, don't we?"

We drove to El Bucanero, at the edge of the sea. The wind was blowing hard as we stepped out of the car.

"I hope a northerly isn't brewing," he said.

I shuddered. Rafael had told me that this was the period for northerlies and no one has forgotten the effects of Hurricane Roxanne.

The restaurant was full, so we waited at the bar for a while. When we got a table, I was hungry for the first time in many days. Miguel ordered crab claws and I, grilled shrimp.

There I was, eating and drinking with a man I had just met, talking about my life as if I had to confess it in order to exorcise it. Miguel listened attentively. He asked me the usual things: what I did, who I was married to… I talked about Rafael, my children, my work. I even had the brilliant idea of bursting into tears. I couldn't avoid it. "I'm going to cry," I told myself, "I have no right to be happy. Miguel will pity me and I can't accept that." But my tears rolled out anyway, perhaps out of exhaustion or too much drink.

"What's wrong?"

"Nothing."

"Open up. This is your chance."

Miguel called the waiter, ordered another bottle of wine and lit a cigarette which he put to my lips. And while we drank the wine, I told him about Eduardo. I had to tell someone, I had held it in much too long. Miguel listened respectfully, but every once in a while he'd tease me to get me to smile.

I told him that Eduardo was a cardiologist, a student of Dr. Chávez to whom he owed his career. I never read the biography he wrote about his teacher, I tried, but it was much too boring. Eduardo was always referring to his teacher:

I've been preparing my talk on "The Moral Role of Doctors and the Training of New Doctors at the Turn of the 21st Century" for the Conference of Cardiologists in New York. My colleagues at the New York Academy suggested the topic and I must confess I don't like it much. Who am I to speak of morality, when I hate being a moralist? And still, I must set out the main points of a professional ethos and fine tune them from time to time, in accordance with changes in the medical profession, society and judicial regulations.

I decided to address the risk to the patient of experimenting with new drugs instead of talking about medical secrets or the dilemma of being both a medical official and a confidante. I knew that despite myself I would begin by citing my teacher, Dr. Chávez: "With individual ethics as a guide, the doctor will almost always find his way."

Chávez was a great doctor, as you know, without ever relinquishing his authority. That's why I said in my biography that he was contradictory. He was part of a generation that modernized cardiology in Mexico, passing from auscultation and the stethoscope to electrocardiograms, x-rays, clinical lab analysis...His generation developed treatment and prevention, research and teaching.

Chávez's boldness did not consist solely of training doctors and enforcing changes in the Medical School and the General Hospital. By founding the National Institute of Cardiology, he achieved not only technical and scientific advancements, but also humanized medical practice; for him, the attitude toward the patient was equal to excellence in medical treatment. He taught us to read, to draw pleasure from the arts. He saw everything as going hand-in-hand with medicine.

I have never wanted to criticize Chávez: he threw himself into the study, treatment and surgical procedures of heart disease with young cardiologists like myself—people he himself sent abroad to train with those in the international vanguard. But it can't be denied that he held great power within our trade association. His group alone, of which I was a part, dominated the hospitals and teaching schools. He would enforce his will, with style. He was a forthright, honest, respectable, unswerving man but he had his vision and he imposed it upon us. Wherever he went he was the one who was in command. He had quite a talent for imposing his will, and though he was a fair and reasonable person, he was emotional and forceful in his power. Do you understand?

Wasn't Eduardo becoming exactly like the man he criticized? I told Miguel about the Eduardo who had seduced me with his letters and had been careful with his appointments, his way of being, his passion. Why had I found him so late in life? It wasn't as if I didn't love Rafael. I was pregnant when we married, but I loved him... And yet it had been a different kind of affection. Maybe because I was older and more mature, the passion I felt for Eduardo was unyielding. I had never been ready to change my life, not even when he assured me he could no longer live with his wife:

My dream is to separate from Ilona and live with you. In the last few months I have wanted to find a way to leave her, but a separation, no matter how it works out, isn't so easy.

"Eduardo told me he was getting a divorce. But I never considered marrying him."

"What happened to the prince happened to him," Miguel teased me.

"What prince?"

"From a story told by a friend of mine."

"What story?"

"It begins where others leave off: '...and the prince and the princess married. And everything seemed to be going well. The king received a letter every week from his daughter telling him that she was very happy. But the letters began coming less frequently: once a month, then every six months. The king was surprised to hear that the princess now complained that life was unfair. The years went by, and the king heard no more news, until one afternoon he received a message: the princess wanted an immediate divorce.

'The king called his ministers and after consulting with them, got on his horse and set out toward the palace where his daughter lived. When he arrived, the prince spoke to him politely and warmly:

'Your Majesty is most welcome. It is a pleasure to have you with us.'"

Despite my gloom, Miguel made me smile. He drama-tized the story as if he were reading a tale from *A Thousand and One Nights*. I had lit a cigarette and was puffing away pleasurably, watching his grand gestures, trying to figure out how the story would end.

"'I understand, your Majesty,' the prince continued, 'that my wife has complained to you about our marriage. I will respect whatever she says to you. I won't say a word for a week. You are in your palace, your Majesty. I only wish to ask you one question. I would like to attend to you, as you deserve. Please tell me: what is your favorite dish?'

'Lobster,' the king answered, surprised by the strange question.

'I will see you at dinner, your Majesty.'

During the meal the king enjoyed the most delicious lobster he had ever eaten in his lengthy gourmet's life. The prince didn't say a word.

The following morning the king was served lobster again. During lunch and dinner he once more ate lobster. The king, immensely satisfied, took great pleasure in the exquisite dishes.

For a week the king ate lobster prepared in a variety of ways. The prince still said nothing.

When the week ended, the king spoke first:

'How is it that you serve me lobster morning, noon and night?'

'Your Majesty,' the prince replied. 'You told me it was your favorite food.'

'But you can't eat it at every meal,' the king complained, growing angry.

'Then you must understand, Your Majesty,' the prince countered, 'what is ailing me: princess in the morning, princess at noon, princess at night.'"

Miguel's joke had distracted me.

"Do you have a girlfriend?" I asked him.

"We're hearing your story, not mine."

I told Miguel just about everything that had happened with Eduardo and a little bit about our trip to New York, when Eduardo had gone to give his talk on future medical ethics. We had planned our trip to New York together, and I told Rafael that the ad agency was sending me to meet a client.

I also told Miguel about the letters of our breakup:

This is a difficult letter to write. You are a bright woman and I am sure you will understand. I love you, but I am sure that you have realized that our relationship, the way it is now, cannot continue. I am twenty years your senior, Marcela. I can only offer you, as you have witnessed, my collapse, my decline, old age. On the other hand, you are a young woman, with much living ahead of you. Love isn't everything. Especially this kind of love, Marcela, based more on dreams than on reality.

He was wrong. Eduardo was wrong—my love was not based on dreams, it was real.

Miguel watched me for a few seconds, then said: "Another Eduardo will appear, don't worry."

The words "Another Eduardo will appear" stayed etched in my mind.

"Not all of us, Miguel, are rich in spirit, loyal, or lucky. I'm tired of thinking, tired of remembering and still I go on thinking and remembering. I continue thinking and remembering, and I'm still set on making Eduardo love me. What good does it do me? I should forget him, but I can't. I simply can't."

"It's okay," Miguel answered. "Why forgot something that was delightful? You only need to understand that it *was* and won't continue to be. You came out the winner."

I felt like vomiting, more from drinking too much than from anguish. I had been drinking those past few days as if it were my job. My only task.

"Let's get out of here," I said.

"Sure. I'll take you to the waterfront so you can sober up a bit. Then I'll take you to see what San Lázaro is like at night."

"A better San Lázaro than we've seen?"

"If not better, more entertaining," Miguel laughed, gesturing to the waiter to bring him the check.

Chapter Twelve

I don't know how long we walked along the waterfront, but I do remember that it was deserted. No cars drove down the avenue, perhaps because of the late hour or because everyone had gone to bed, chased away by the wind blowing so strongly it made the dry fronds of the palm trees sound like rattlesnakes.

"Is it a northerly?"

"If it were we wouldn't be here."

"But isn't this an omen?"

Miguel's thick longish hair flopped from one side of his head to the other, and I had had to take a clasp from my purse to hold mine in place. His voice was a bit hoarse, probably from trying to keep the wind from carrying away his words. He asked probing questions, not respecting my privacy, as if searching for my secret soul—the part that only bursts out when one is alone or in a confessional, so he could put my thoughts or my life in order. What I had never confessed to anyone, I now did to Miguel, unburdening myself.

Who was Miguel? Why had we met? I thought he might want to sleep with me, but he never tried to seduce me. Or maybe it was his way of seducing. Anyway, I kept my eyes wide open: I didn't want to wrap up my visit to San Lázaro involved in a pointless affair.

"I don't get it? What happened in New York?" he shouted.

The wind cleared my head enough so I could see myself as if I were someone else, someone not inside of me, someone who I once was without knowing it.

"Nothing."

"What?"

"Nothing. Can't you hear?" I said, annoyed.

"Why does that *nothing* hurt you?"

What happened in New York was that Eduardo broached his intention to break off the affair. It came out of the blue and was like waiting for the phone to ring after a long, hurtful silence but when it does, it's not the call you've been waiting for. Now you can't tell him about a movie you saw, a book you read, a conversation you had with someone he knows; now you won't be making a date, now the letter you expect won't arrive, and you don't know what to do with your emotions and affections that don't fit anywhere because you can't share them with anyone because they're in the way, because the interest and fondness for your husband and children is something different, totally distinct.

Apparently, journeys sometimes lead nowhere. Instead of having foreseen the break up or been the one to initiate it, I became a victim of my own desires, the prey of my own insecurity and fear.

I arrived in New York on the morning of the last day of Eduardo's conference and checked into the Hotel Beacon on Broadway and 75th Street, near Central Park. This was two weeks before our first attempted breakup and three from our second—just after Raúl Salinas de Gortarti was arrested, accused of killing José Francisco Ruiz Massieu which put the Mexican political situation into complete turmoil.

Everyone followed each new chapter of Mexico's soap opera in the newspapers and on television. All conversations focused on it and also on the tense standoff in Chiapas. Rafael was sought out by *Chiapanecos* for his advice to sue peasants for having seized private lands or to sue the same old *caciques* for confiscating the belongings of those Indians displaced from their lands. He was called for every illegal arrest or disappearance—Rafael had connections and could investigate as well as mediate.

Whenever Rafael came back from Chiapas, he'd be tired and depressed and would discuss with other *Chiapanecos* his theories about the conflict: the struggle between the right-wing, conservative Church and the left, which he referred to as the progressive sector, the one working in the communities. He talked about how religious syncretism gave strength, by way of its idiosyncratic spiritual rituals, to the people's struggles. He'd underscore the economic inequities in Chiapas and go on to say that the peasants who had joined the guerrilla movement were self-educated Indians who had learned a lot from rural self-rule policies. He'd mention the Maoists who had failed to take root and were not accepted by the Indians, and the guerrillas of Comandante Marcos's generation whom he referred to as creative Marxists.

Rafael's obsession was Chiapas and his office life. He mentioned "Marcos" and "Father Samuel Ruiz" more than his own children's, or even my own, name.

I believe I've already mentioned that St. Mark was one of my mother's favorites:

Hearken; Behold, there went out a sower to sow: and it came to pass as he sowed, some fell by the wayside, and the fowls of the air came and devoured it up. And some fell on stony ground, where it had not much earth...

"The seeds of St. Mark," she'd say to Rafael, half seriously, half in jest, "fell on the land of the poor and began to grow."

To me, Marcos was a religious person. Back then he was extremely popular and had a strong presence in the media. Women of all classes admired him. The slogan "We are all Marcos" began to spread. Not me—I wasn't Marcos and couldn't pretend I was. He was a fighter—"leave everything behind and follow me"—while I, despite my name, was no warrior. The office secretaries were crazy about him and he was the idol of many college girls. My sister-in-law Margarita had his picture in her bedroom. I'd tease her by saying: "When he finds out you're a landowner, he won't accept you in his ranks."

In his trips back to Chiapas, Rafael worked for whoever needed him, whether he was paid with a hen or a pig, which he accepted so as not to offend and then left it with a relative, or he was not paid at all. He was morally committed to help his countrymen put an end to the conflict somehow. So he flew back and forth to Tuxtla Gutiérrez and paid little attention to my New York trip, perhaps because things at home were in order. Pancho could take care of any domestic issue that arose in my absence. Rafael was also unaware of any change in mood after my trip. Knowing that the Indians trusted Rafael, the Chiapas government had asked him, through a friend, to join the negotiations. Rafael declined; he preferred to mediate freely and maintain his independence.

Eduardo had chosen the Beacon because it was a nice place, not normally frequented by Mexicans traveling to New York; the suites are very popular with European businessmen. He didn't want us running into anyone.

The reservation was under Eduardo's name. When I signed the hotel register a girl, who spoke Spanish in a nondescript accent, told me that my husband would be back in the evening, that he had checked in early so everything would be set for my arrival. I walked happily and calmly toward the elevator. It was the first time I wasn't plagued or embarrassed to lie about my amorous relationship with Eduardo. I was confident I deserved that legroom—that affection and friendship—in my life.

We were given a spacious, comfortable suite on the 10th floor, with a view of Manhattan's East Side. Bedroom, huge living room with sash windows, and modern, cozy kitchen-ette with a bar that faced the living room. I found a fruit bowl with apples, plums and peaches. On the living room table there was a bouquet of flowers and, on the bed, Eduardo's welcome:

> I dread
> not measuring up
> to you,
> to what you are expecting.

I picked up the card and read it several times, pacing back and forth in the room, before putting it away. I remembered the note he had given me the day we had run off to Metepec:

> It's too late
> to start a life
> between us;
> but between
> the two of us,
> we can slowly
> sketch this bit
> of life we share.

Weren't we carefully sketching this bit of life? What did I want from Eduardo? Until then, I hadn't asked myself that question. I hoped to be with him for an entire day followed by an entire night, and so on and so on, till we had spent 3 days and 3 nights together. I honestly believed—with the simplemindedness or confidence or lack of foresight that characterizes me—that this would be the beginning of a new and better stage in our relationship, a test case. Evidently, Eduardo hadn't passed the test he had imposed upon himself or he flunked me without letting me know. What did he want from me? I still can't answer that question. Honestly, I believed that he wanted someone who could calm his soul, be patient and tender with him. Because I loved him, none of that was hard for me.

I knew that he wouldn't be free till nine at night, so I unpacked and went out for a walk and to have lunch. I walked across 57th Street to Fifth Avenue, looking into the window displays, at the neon ads on the marquees, at the faces of people who see nothing but the person right in front of them or who walk lost in their own thoughts.

Suddenly I thought of my mother, always so locked up, so lonely. She never went further than Tabasco and San Lázaro, because Cuernavaca and the San Juan Teotihuacán spa, where we'd go on vacations, was by then so close to Mexico City that you could get there by bus in an hour and a half or less. In San Juan Teotihuacán we learned to swim and to dive from the 15 foot diving board into the Olympic-size swimming pool. The grounds were vast, the climate blissful. The spa filled up with families who brought huge baskets of ham and cheese or chicken sandwiches, bottled beer and soft drinks, making it their picnic.

We wouldn't eat there but go instead to the archeological zone nearby where my parents bought me tiny clay casseroles and pots from the craft stands. My brothers and I would climb the pyramids while my parents stayed below making small talk wherever they could find a bit of shade, sitting comfortably on the *serape* my mother brought for the occasion. Then we'd have lunch in La Gruta, a restaurant owned by Luis Cedillo, a friend of my father with whom he'd smoke cigars smelling of forests, drink *Presidente* brandy and converse as if they'd known each other since childhood. Then we'd go off to play or look for pieces of obsidian or clay—*tepalcates* his son Luis Cedillo called them, just shards that you could find all over the place. Once I even found a tiny woman's head that I still have. Or we'd go back to the archeological zone to see the frescoes or go horseback riding with Mr. Cedillo's children. There was nothing I liked more than to ride in the saddle of Luis's pinto—he was fourteen and I was twelve. I'd ride through corn and alfalfa fields and let him tell me that I was his girl and that he would come get me in Mexico City when we were older so we could live together in San Juan. Back then I longed for our vacations so we could run freely through the orchards, the farms and the arable lands, and this drove off the oppression that often came over me. It was great to play under a sun that tanned our bodies while we swam, rode horseback, or hung a swing from the branches of Mexican cypresses or red peppers and took turns on it. Luis made sure that I had plenty of turns.

Sometimes it was nearly impossible to get our father to stop talking and drinking with Don Luis. My mother would tell my brother Juan: "Tell your dad to say good-bye to Mr. Cedillo. It's late, almost night, and we have to walk over to the bus station."

My mother always had us bring messages to our father, something that drove me nuts.

My mother never crossed the Mexican border and I don't know if even once in her life she dreamed of escaping her fate. I tried to get close to her, for the first time, when she was sick in our house. It happened on the night I was reading a verse from the *Gospel According to St. John*, which she had requested:

Jesus said unto her, Woman, where are those thine accusers? Hath no man condemned thee? She said, No man, Lord…

"Again. Please read that part again," she murmured.

And Jesus said unto her, Neither do I condemn thee…

I wondered why she had asked me to read that verse from St. John. I tried to understand her, to forgive her compliance, her resignation.

Before she fell asleep I dared to ask: "I need you to tell me something."

She opened her eyes.

"Did you know that Father had another family?"

She closed her eyes.

"Did you know?"

Looking at her I felt I did not know my mother. I knew little more than that she had a certain talent with plants and animals: she would take cuttings from saplings and they'd root and flower. She raised chickens on the roof and canaries in the courtyard, and would have bought a dog if our house hadn't been so modest and had included a garden. Neighbors sought her out for her skill with medicinal plants which she must've inherited from her mother. She knew how to heal with massages, herbal teas, and special diets. She suggested white zapote juice for insomnia, lemon blossom tea for rabies, a teaspoonful of olive oil for bilious conditions, swatches of basil for cold sores, starch for abrasions...She knew the properties of many herbs, and she would rub down my brothers with rosemary and rue leaves wherever they hurt themselves playing soccer.

However, I knew nothing of her inner life. I didn't know what ailed her, what she liked, what she hated, what worried her, what her childhood had been like, what she remembered of Tabasco, what her life had been like when she had married my father and they fled San Lázaro, what she felt when she learned of his betrayal.... Did she feel lonely without her family? After her parents died, she almost never saw any other relatives. I don't remember meeting an uncle or cousin of either of my parents—they all remained behind in Tabasco or San Lázaro. Sometimes some distant relative of my mother would come from Tabasco, but soon leave. I knew almost nothing about my mother, and she wasn't going to live forever, especially in her condition. "She's going to die and we never became close," I thought.

"Why won't you tell me?"

"Hmmm."

"Are you ashamed?"

"I didn't know."

"Did you forgive him?"

She shut her eyes again.

"Tell me."

I didn't insist. It was her secret. Since she never confided in me, I couldn't expect her to suddenly open her heart to me.

Sometimes I try to understand my father, to forgive him. Maybe he was right in trying to have something my mother couldn't give him. But why didn't he tell her? Why didn't they separate or divorce? The deception is what hurt us. Deception is what hurts me: my betrayal of Rafael, Eduardo's cowardice. We know that infidelity is the staff of life; but no one thinks beforehand of the damage it leaves behind. I've asked myself if my father's way of being hadn't somehow seeped into my own body unawares.

I had gone to New York several times with Rafael and felt uncomfortable when recalling walking the streets with him, going to Central Park, buying clothes for our children, watching the Rockefeller Center skaters or having a drink at the Plaza before going to dinner, the theater or a movie.

During our last visit we hadn't seen so many crazy people talking alone and aloud on the streets, nor so many destitute men and women. I glanced around me: people walked in and out of the subways and shops, crossed the streets obeying the traffic lights and pushed along as they went like a flock of goats rushing in a pack.

I bought a few dresses and blouses at Casual Corner, three outfits at Ann Taylor, after trying them on and wondering if Eduardo would like them. I thought of my mother again, felt hurt by the deception and capriciousness, and imagined her—she whose checkered apron was the only item she ever replaced—reproaching me not only for my purchases, but for my reasons for buying them.

And I answered her as if she could hear me: "No one is free of guilt, Mother. No one."

When I was finally exhausted, I went into an Italian restaurant and had a pasta and salad before taking a cab back to the hotel. I set the alarm for eight and fell into the kind of deep sleep that exhaustion and the unconscious sometimes permit you.

I had taken a shower and put on my makeup when Eduardo arrived—just what was in the cards.

I was waiting for him with the TV on though I wasn't watching it but rather wondering how we would greet, how we would find one another. I was scared. I looked at my watch: "He'll be here in 30 minutes, in 23 minutes, he'll walk through the door in 15…"

He calmly hung up his raincoat and when he embraced me, we embarked on a new stage of life for both of us.

The city hid us for three days; meanwhile I observed Eduardo and felt observed by him. I began recognizing myself in him as if he were someone I had forgotten and he were there to remind me who I was. So I rediscovered my body and let him unlock the door into my abandoned corners and realize his fantasies. I was the lighthouse and the safe harbor for his boat, and I guided him so he could go fearlessly all the way to my shores.

I explored the secrets of his everyday life during those days, with the help of his luggage and his toilet bag. I learned which medicines he took, what deodorant he preferred, his favorite shaving cream, the toothpaste he used, and I had his comb in my hands and I put on his hair gel. I also inspected the brand of his underwear; he wore boxers instead of briefs. I could buy him any item of clothes since I knew the size of his collar and shirtsleeves, the waist and length of his pants, his shoe size… At the same time, I was conquering his body, memorizing every detail. I still remember little things like the birth mark on his right forearm. I watched him sleep and counted the age spots on his back or looked at the belly age had given him, a paunch that Rafael will have in time. I admired the length of his legs tanned by the Cuernavaca sun or the scar which spoiled his left buttock, a scar that had resulted from a poor inoculation which had led to an operation when he was a boy. I watched how he shaved, brushed his teeth, combed himself, dressed and undressed. While I took off my makeup or put on my nightgown, he tuned in the news or old movies. He would always order cereal and fruit for breakfast, never eggs. He usually had fish or chicken for lunch, and generally a light dinner. I followed him curiously in bookstores: he liked mysteries, novels by contemporary American and European authors, but he could also buy photography, art, or film books. He also liked biographies, just like my father who loved them. I can still remember the books and records he bought: Frank Sinatra's *Gold Collection*, music of Irving Berlin, George Gershwin and Cole Porter, *100 Years of Cinema*...He's a fanatic of jazz, blues, the music of the twenties, thirties and forties.

Eduardo bought a CD player. My biggest dream was to dance with him. "I don't like to dance, I don't know how to," he told me, but if I close my eyes, I feel him embracing me, carrying me off to a dream world from which I still can't escape. So I learned about the music of those eras. I learned to appreciate Ella Fitzgerald, Sarah Vaughan, Billie Holiday, Judy Garland, Ginger Rogers and Betty Hutton. Dying of laughter, I listened to Eduardo accompany Cole Porter and sing *You're the Top* and then dance like Fred Astaire:

> ...you're the top,
> you're the Coliseum,
> you're the top,
> you're the Louvre Museum

you're a melody from a symphony by
Strauss...

I also noticed that, like my father, Eduardo suffered
some from urinary incontinence, perhaps due to a prostate
problem he never discussed with me and I did not question
him about. It was so obvious because he would get up from
his movie seat and go to the bathroom, sometimes twice, or
he would go to the bathroom whenever we came into or left
a place.

During those days I observed him left and right, with a
strange mixture of fear and attraction for the part of him I
didn't know and with astonishment and desire that seemed
excessive, even to me.

During the day we wouldn't go to the museums—not
the Metropolitan, the Guggenheim, the Jewish Museum, nor
the Museum of the City of New York. We were afraid to run
into people we knew so, instead—though we could meet
people there as well—we walked through Chinatown, Little
Italy, Greenwich Village, Soho or further north, through
Columbia University and Riverside Park. We wouldn't go to
the Lincoln Center cinemas, but to those in Queens and
Brooklyn. We also avoided any Broadway plays because
Eduardo feared someone would see us there. So I lived the
misfortune of moving in the shadows, despite the distance
from our families. I'd love it if you came to Paris with me,
he'd say, and I would nod my head in silence, letting him
dream on...

Eduardo was so devoted and affectionate to me during
that trip that now I recognize it as a prelude to our breakup
or just plain guilt. Before going to sleep, I listened to him—
dazzled by the novelty—tell me his life story from the beginning, from his childhood in Metepec to his "unbearable"
relationship with Ilona. When I told Eduardo that I had met
her at an art opening, he grew restless. I could tell that he
didn't like that.

I understood Eduardo's expression when he evoked the events that had marked him for life. I grew closer to him by learning not only about his happy moments but also the violence, the humiliation, the impulsive or impetuous acts, the intense moments he had endured.

I told him about my childhood, too, my adolescence, when I had played with dolls, played cars with my brothers, or recited in school the Espronceda poem: "*Bajel pirata que llaman por su bravura El Temido, en todo el mar conocido, del uno al otro confín...*" or when I played *Clair de Lune* on the school piano, without knowing that he existed and that one day I would finally meet this Meek Pirate, much too late, and would tell him how nervous I was in starting the piece and how I tried to please the teacher so she wouldn't tell my father that I had no musical talent because I felt that he would love me only for my music, given that I wasn't submissive or a conformist like my mother but difficult, hard to understand, unruly like all the Souzas. I lived in my own world full of all sorts of dreams, and he could not break me even if he sent me to my room and wouldn't let me out to hear his records or phone my girlfriends back.

I was surprised to remember little details that I had forgotten. For example, my recurrent dreams where I was underage but drove a car or flew over the city. I always have dreams with cars in them, with driving, perhaps to steer my own life. I told Eduardo about my father's dying in the house of his other wife; his burial on a gloomy, rainy morning in June. About how we didn't know how to act now that two intruders had entered the scene; about my disastrous brothers, as my mother referred to them; about my timid and innocent stepbrothers who had no idea of their father's betrayal and felt so resentful for being the children, the forgotten ones, from his second home.

I loved Eduardo during those days. I was patient, tender and understanding; and his closeness filled everything with a delicate, transparent happiness like a baby's laughter. I heard him say more than twice that he was going to divorce Ilona and live with me.

"And if I don't get divorced?" I'd asked.

"Well, I'm going to live with you even though you don't believe me," he deceived himself.

Miguel took me by the arm. We walked toward his car and he suggested that we go out dancing.

"In this wind?"

"It's dying down."

"I don't think so."

"Are you not allowed to go dancing?"

"Where do you want to go?"

"Somewhere to enjoy ourselves. You certainly need it."

"I'm tired," I replied, afraid. It was too hard to be with Miguel.

"You'll rest soon enough."

We drove through the red-light district, not a very long street, but depraved and terrible.

"We shouldn't have come this way, but it's part of San Lázaro…so you'll have a full picture of the city, since you didn't get one from your grandfather," he said mockingly.

After driving down and seeing from the car that secret land of faces, thighs, and breasts in the display windows of the early morning, after passing entryway after entryway covered with curtains like war flags or else open, where loud salsa music rushed out, and the cheapest drinking holes, we went to a dance hall called La Manzana.

It stank of cheap tobacco and sweat, had either red or blue lights, depending on the strobe on the dance floor. But the women were neither common nor vulgar, but healthy and happy, spontaneous in their pleasure and attitude, quite natural. There were young and older women, some prettier and more voluptuous than others. They greeted Miguel warmly—no doubt he was a regular visitor there. Suddenly

I recovered my trust in him because his face was so transparent; perhaps it was his sense of humor, his laughter, his kindness. He is an honest and kind man.

They brought us a couple of beers.

"To the past," Miguel toasted, "that can never be recovered nor relived."

When we left, the sun had risen and the wind had died down. He drove his car down the streets of a city that I never would have known without him. We drove up and down wide or narrow streets or along cobblestone roads till we reached the beach. Seagulls flew across the sky.

I took off my shoes and walked on the sand, Miguel next to me, as if he were my guardian angel.

Chapter Thirteen

When I picked up my room key at reception, I was handed several phone messages and Miguel's yellow folder. Rafael had called me three times; I went upstairs, dead-tired and sleepy, to call him back.

"I didn't think I'd catch you, Rafael."

"Where have you been?"

"With some friends."

"You didn't know anyone."

"I made friends and we went out for dinner."

"Where?"

"What's the difference? You don't know the place."

"Where did you go?"

"Rafael…"

"I called you early this morning. You weren't in."

"I went down for breakfast," I lied.

"With some friends?"

"Rafael…"

"Pancho will pick you up at the airport."

"I'd like you to."

"I can't."

"Please come."

"Marcela…"

"I'll see you at the airport."

"Another whim of yours."

"Hmmm."

"I have a meeting with Ramón Suárez."

"You choose," I answered, hanging up.

I really wanted to see Rafael. Foolish as it sounds, his unease at not finding me made me realize he loved me. As if I didn't know. But you like to hear the words "I love you." I suddenly missed him. I imagined myself wrapped up in his legs, embraced by his arms, in the safety of my home, my room, my bed. Can you understand?

The phone rang. I guessed it was Rafael, upset by my ploy.

"I'll come by to take you to the airfield," said Miguel.

"To where?"

"To the airfield."

"That's what they call airports in old war movies."

"Well, that's what we still call it in San Lázaro. I'll be in your lobby at 5:15 p.m. Get some rest."

We had had a breakfast of pork tacos *pibil* and rice milkshakes in the main market. The market was enormous, very clean and filled with the aroma of fruit, oregano, bay leaves, achiote, Spanish onions and the sea.

Despite all the supermarkets, the Indians still come down to the harbor to bring their fruits and vegetables to market, and they lay their Havana chiles, beans, rice and corn on white blankets and sell them by the dry quarter liter and not by the kilo. The women talk to you in the informal "tu" form while nursing their children: "Do you want to take a quarter?"

We happily walked by the stands, while the merchants sliced their fruit and gave us samples of the sweet, juicy meat of sapodilla, mango and custard apple; or others would call us over to see the red snapper, dogfish, porgies and pompanos fresh off the boats; still others would have us breathe in the aromatic fragrances of *bucayo* lilies, horse reeds, mimosas, buttercups, Christ's crown and dahlias… It seemed you could get all the flowers in the world in San Lázaro… We were dragged over to see cloth brought from who knows where or hand embroidered dresses or closed-stitch cotton or open-stitched woven hammocks in the wild colors that the tourists preferred... Miguel bought a bottle of plum and cashew syrup at a stand that sold spirits and fruit preserves.

"For when your kids come back."

And he took me to the best guayabera stand in San Lázaro.

"Your husband will thank you."

"Pancho will thank me."

"Who's he?"

"The peacemaker of the house."

I would have brought Eduardo a balsam leaf to place inside one of his books.

When we got back to my hotel, I was sure that Miguel would invent any excuse to come up to my room. I felt my back begin to stiffen, but Miguel simply gave me a kiss on the cheek and said: "If you lived here, I would marry you."

"Thanks for everything."

"Not all women are lucky enough to experience what you have."

"You call it luck?"

"Of course."

"To suffer like that?"

"Another Eduardo will appear. I told you that..."

"God help me!"

"Accept who you are."

Honestly, I had never thought of that. To accept myself for what I am, freeing myself to explore the depths of my passion. Suddenly I shuddered.

I didn't ask Miguel for his address or phone number. I knew it wouldn't be difficult to find him, if I wanted to—I just needed to seek out Sra. Canto in the Archbishop's Archives—but the magic would be gone.

I took a bath, deciding to face Eduardo's letters once

and for all. Otherwise I wouldn't be able to leave San Lázaro. Spades:

> *...I trust in your generosity and your forgiveness.*
> *Lovingly,*
> *Eduardo.*

Chapter Fourteen

A few days after my return from San Lázaro, I got a call from Ilona Soskay. What do you do when your hands shake so much you can't grasp the phone?

"Are you sure, María?"

"That's what she said. Ilona Soskay."

"Really?"

My heart pounded as if awaiting the results of a pregnancy test or for the doctor to come out of the operating room to tell you the results of your child's surgery or when you wake up, troubled by a nightmare that grips you and haunts you and recurs whenever it wants.

Lately I've dreamt that I am at the movies and suddenly I find Eduardo sitting in front of me, but I don't know if he is alone or with the girl to his right. I don't want him to know I'm there, watching the same movie, but each of us is suffering in his own solitude. I don't like the film, the violence makes me sad and fearful. I want to walk out, but Rafael's firm hand holds me back.

Her clear voice without an accent upset me. The paralyzing fear disappeared little by little as Ilona spoke to me. She had asked Juan Manuel for my telephone number and called me a few times without success. She was going to curate an exhibit of textiles in San Antonio, Texas, and wanted me to sell her my mother's *rebozo*, definitely a collector's item. She also wanted me to design the catalog.

I felt such sorrow and resentment toward Ilona!

I had decided not to think of Eduardo, not to go to any place where I could bump into him, to change my routine at the office so I wouldn't notice that the phone wasn't ringing at ten or six. I had been working full-time from the moment my kids went away to school. I did all this, cancelled everything, even my P.O. box. I truly wanted to expel him from my world. I even stopped hurting myself—I gave up smoking and drinking on impulse, that's what it had become—forgoing an occasional glass of wine and a cigarette. I was also going to the gym to sweat out my grief. But suddenly Ilona's voice brought me to a distant and unexplored place, where desire, guilt, dissatisfaction and suffering awaited me. A place where I still concealed the feelings I had been incapable of destroying and which, just then, pushed against my chest. I felt both sad and happy, simply to hear something about Eduardo even if Ilona hadn't even mentioned his name.

She was urging me to name my price for my mother's *rebozo* though she knew perfectly well its real value. She even had the nerve to say that the *rebozo* should be properly cared for and not allowed to deteriorate. Ilona also wanted me to prepare a dummy of the exhibit catalog for the directors of the San Antonio Museum. That way I could make a few *pesitos*—that's how she said it, very Mexican-like.

"I wasn't brought up to make money or to be faithful, Ilona," I said in jest, amused by the irony.

"Money doesn't hurt. As the saying goes: it's easier to put up with pain on a full stomach."

While listening to her, I realized I could give Ilona something else. Not out of guilt but because I can be as wicked as my grandfather or as generous as my mother who, though she wouldn't confess it to me, forgave my father. If you hold in resentment, you won't age gracefully.

I couldn't help myself. "How is the doctor doing?"

"Wanting to retire," is all she said.

This Ilona with her raging menopause, bedroom separate from Eduardo's, legs closed, selfish and ambitious, frustrated, frowning, jealous, and neurotic...Ilona, with everything going against the odds of making someone happy, still had Eduardo at her side.

I asked her to forgive me for turning down the offer to do the dummy, but I had too much work. I also told her she could pick up the *rebozo,* that it was my gift to her. All remorse carries penitence with it.

Days later I had my just reward: Pancho asked me where he should put my mother's suitcase. I had asked him to put my mother's furniture in the sewing room on the second floor so I could fix up the study for my boys who were about to return.

"What suitcase, Pancho?"

"I had forgotten all about it."

"Forgotten what?"

"The suitcase I had stored under your mother's bed."

"Under her bed?"

"That's where doña Lolita asked me to put it. She said that she wanted to go through it later..."

"Can you bring it here?"

It was locked, of average size but extremely heavy. I couldn't remember my mother having a small key among her things, but I went to get the key ring she had brought from her apartment and gave it to Pancho to see if any of the keys worked. Pancho ended up using wire, pliers and a screwdriver, but as he couldn't open it, he simply smashed the lock.

The suitcase was full of papers. Jesus! At the top were electric, telephone, real estate and water bills from 1954. I also found her telephone book, addresses written in pencil in her old-fashioned script, some of father's IDs from Pasquel Brothers Customs Agency, a few manila envelopes...I shut the suitcase and asked Pancho to bring it to the den and leave it next to the table. I figured that later that night, while waiting for Rafael, I'd go through the papers to see what I should save. Then I went into my children's study.

"How's it going, Pancho?"

"It needs another coat of paint."

I'm sure that Pancho also missed the boys. They would be returning very soon...When Rafael suggested that I could go pick them up, I argued that we should go together. I wanted to reconnect with him. Something like starting over. At least try.

That night I put a trashcan near the table and began sifting through the papers in the suitcase. How can anyone save so much garbage? Mother had even saved some old laundry receipts.

What was my great-grandfather's certificate doing there? It had a coat-of-arms, with castles and galley ships, and a flowery script, especially in the signatures. Still I could read the words.

In the Parish Seminary of the Archangel Miguel de Estrada in the Liberal city and port of San Lázaro, on the twenty-third day of the month of August in the year 1827, the following individuals, as was their custom, came together: SS.LL. Dr. Prefecto Mateos, President of the Board of Examiners; Dr. Eduardo Raymundo Valles, representative of the synod; Dr. Eduardo María Rojo, Professor of Jurisprudence; and I, the undersigned scribe and synod member, to judge the candidacy of Dr. Leandro J. Souza, the fourth year student in Juris-prudence, who discussed Natural Law, the Elements of Burlamaqui, Civil Law, the History of Roman, Spanish and Mexican Law, the Elucidation of the Royal Law of Spain *written by D. Juan Sala with an appendix as a conclusion; and also representing the Canonical Law, all of Cavalario's Canonical Law. And having been completely interrogated, he received an evaluation of Excellent by Unanimous Vote.*

Joining me as witness were Prefecto Mateos, Eduardo R. Valles, Eduardo María Rojo and Tomás Pérez Blanco, Secretary.

Why would my father save this document? Probably more as a good-luck charm than a relic. Maybe it was his only bond with his family. Perhaps because his grandfather had been a lawyer and my father never completed his law studies. But how did he get hold of it?

I also found father's Social Security application, some savings bonds, grocery coupons, recipes written in my mother's hand, some 1938 pennies and 1960 five-peso coins. Buttons and empty boxes and tinfoil—lots of tinfoil perhaps stretched smooth with a fingernail—the kind of foil used to wrap chocolates, with descriptive vignettes that will never be read again. Bank deposits, check stubs, invitations to the wedding of friends and people I did not know...

I found in one of the envelopes pictures of my brothers and of me: a toothless Juan laughing astride a tricycle that I'd forgotten we had; Alberto dressed as a Veracruz native, perhaps for a school function; Juan and Alberto in swim suits at the San Juan Teotihuacán spa; Alberto in shorts holding my father's hand in Alameda Park; Alberto, Juan and I with my parents in one of the Xochimilco boats named "Lola"; Alberto and Juan disguised as the Lone Ranger and Tonto and I crying because I didn't have a costume "but girl, you're the one they're going to save." Juan at the Cuernavaca fair with a target rifle in his left hand and a piggybank in his right, a satisfied smile on his face. Perhaps because he was the eldest, he always seemed happy. And I sitting at the piano in the Chopin Room on the afternoon of my first recital. I remember playing Schubert's *Serenade*. On our way to celebrate my performance with tamales and hot chocolate at the Flor de Lis Restaurant my father, instead of congratulating me, told me I hadn't concentrated and played off key. Our weddings, the baptisms of our children, the pictures we had given our parents: "To father, from his loving son Alberto, 1962"; "For mom, with affection from Juan, 1969"; "For mom from Marcela, 1972."

I thought about my brothers and myself, so removed

from that era. I didn't know them anymore, we had become strangers. I didn't know what music they listened to, what sort of films they liked, if they ate everything or had begun to watch their diet, if they had started to lose their hair or gain weight or had begun turning gray, or what they wore as their Sunday best. My mother always scolded Juan because he'd wear the same jeans for weeks. Nor did I know if Alberto still jogged at daybreak or if Juan still played poker on Thursday nights. I knew nothing about them. I put the pictures aside to show Rafael later what my childhood had been like.

In a package wrapped in brown paper, I found other photos and three letters. At first, I thought they were from my parents' friends, but then I realized they were from the family. My heart skipped a beat when I found a photo of my grandfather looking just like my brother Juan. It said "San Lázaro, 1948" on the back. It had to be my grandfather. I wasn't making it up but there was no one to verify it: Juan's eyes, his stare; Juan's smile and mouth; the shape of the face, the way the hair grew...But grandfather with a thick mustache and a beard like one of the Three Wise Men. I was dying of curiosity to find out if my grandmother was there, if I could recognize myself in someone, if they were there, among the eldest, the great-grandparents, or among the youngest, our uncles.

I was suddenly aware that bit by bit I was remembering San Lázaro. I was happy to find it again, reconstruct it in my memory: The San Andrés Church, the Main Square, Bridge Street, the bay, San Fernando Church...

The family was frozen on photographic paper, and yet it was as if it had become blurred in time. Only grandfather existed. They had no names nor any way of recognizing them. As if they had never been born, had no history, nothing concrete that could fix them in the memory of their descendants. Now no one would remember them.

I didn't recognize myself in any of those ghosts but

rather in those things I could touch: I recognized myself in the San Lázaro streets, in that landscape, in that wind ruffling the hair of women, in that heat bearable only in air conditioning, in the still waters of the bay, in the salt stains on the house walls, in the marble floors, in the Marseilles roof tiles. It was the place, not the people, that gave me meaning. Our grandfather had disinherited us from San Lázaro, but I got it back with all the emotions of an exile returning to his homeland. If my father had lived, I would have described to him the many changes in the city he left behind. He wouldn't have believed me had I told him about all those communities on the hills.

I was also unable to separate from my memory that music so out of place in San Lázaro. This bothered me again:

> There was a boy
> a very strange and enchanted boy,
> they say he wandered very far,
> very far, over land and sea...

Why did this music bother me? Because it reminded me of my father, the young man who left everything to go with my mother and then started a second family. Perhaps understanding him, I could begin to understand myself, absolve myself, and repent.

The only pictures I found of my mother's family were the two sepia ovals she kept on her night stand: grandfather with his straw hat tilted to one side and a handlebar mustache and grandmother in a sleeveless dress, her hair in a braid drawn forward and falling across her chest. I hadn't forgotten that picture of my grandmother, solemn or simply frightened by the camera.

I found a 1950 photograph of my mother, with a dedication to my father. Maybe from around the time they were about to leave San Lázaro:

To Leandro. I offer you my love, in exchange for the love you promised me. Will cherish you, always, Dolores.

I felt tenderness, admiration, sadness for my mother. Also happiness for the girl she once was, with her chubby arms and black hair and the smile of a woman in love. I had gone to San Lázaro to search for pictures that were right in my home. How crazy and stupid of me, but I had also found something more.

In letters to her—short notes really, written with little style—I found out that my mother had kept up some kind of contact with my father's family. The letters were undated and without envelopes. By what they said, I could more or less tell when they were written.

• *Dear Lola, I hope this letter finds you all in good health. I'm writing this to let you know I haven't been well on account of Sebastián's wedding. He married Chatita García. Do you remember her? I can't say that it didn't hurt me but, you see, father was not at all pleased by it. How happy you must be there, far away from this house that's just like a jail to me. I hope to hear from you soon. A hug to Leandro and send him my good wishes. Your sister who loves you and misses you. Serafina*

• *Dearest Lola, How are you? I hope that both you and Leandro are well. Herewith you will find the photos of my mother's birthday party you asked me for. I'm a bit chubby, I hope you won't notice. Tell Leandro to please write to me. I beg of him to write me even if it's just a few lines like the ones I send him so that he'll know that I love him and that mother's "boy" has given her a broken heart. Your sister who loves and remembers both of you very much. Serafina*

• *Dear Lola, I hope you are both doing well. I appreciate the news of your pregnancy. I'm dying to meet your firstborn, and I hope he's a boy. By the time you receive this letter—it first must go by boat to Veracruz and then by train to Mexico City—your child will happily have been born, thanks to God the Father and the intervention of my patron saint St. Julius. If I were courageous, I would have already accepted your invitation to live with you. Your sister who loves and wishes you well, Serafina*

If I had known that my father's sister had been in touch with my mother, I wouldn't have been able to give her name to my daughter, if I had had a daughter: that daughter would never have forgiven me.

I examined the photos one by one with a magnifying glass, trying to figure out who they were by their faces, expressions, and wrinkles. I finally recognized Aunt Serafina because she was trying to hide her fatness behind the rocker and had lifeless eyes. Her body reflects her inner tragedy, her unhappiness. And I also recognized my grandmother because she's in the middle of people celebrating something in her honor. She has light transparent eyes and a look similar to Alberto and my father.

I looked again at my grandfather's picture and called Maria. "Tell me, who do you think resembles this man?"

"Your father?"

"No."

"Juan?"

"Doesn't he?"

I wasn't just imagining it or believing that he resembled my brother because that was what I wanted. Maybe that's why my father was so hard on him because Juan reminded him of his own father.

I was so curious to know who was who, dressed in those old-fashioned outfits, in high-collared, pleated dresses and boots, despite the heat... My grandmother was in her rocking chair, in the center, but surrounded by whom? With my mother dead, there were no answers, nothing was clear.

"Why don't you send the pictures to your aunt and uncle in San Lázaro to see if they can identify them?" Rafael suggested.

I thought of Miguel, of sending them to my Miguel and having him research it himself. I looked for the yellow folder he had given me.

It was shocking to read what I found. Maybe it sounds coarse or exaggerated, but it was like reading fragments of *Genesis*:

And Leandro José died before his father José Ignacio, in the land of his birth, the port of San Lázaro. And Santiago and Leandro Manuel took wives for themselves. The name of the wife of Leondro Manuel was Inés, and the name of the wife of Santiago was Carmen, daughter of Domingo, father of Carmen and Hilaria.

And Santiago commanded his son Leandro Marcelo: You will not take a wife from the daughters of any of the immigrants who have found work among us…

Perhaps later, on some afternoon or evening, I will once again feel like looking through my past. Maybe by then I will have forgiven my grandfather, my father, and perhaps, most of all, forgiven myself.

Chapter Fifteen

I know it's hard for anyone to understand me; I can't even say I understand myself. What proof can I offer to justify myself? Nothing. Absolutely nothing. Not even by claiming that we all lack courage, that we're contradictory.

I can't say that, if my father had stayed in San Lázaro, he would have ended up being a lawyer like his father or, perhaps moreso, an honorable and forthright judge. If that had happened, my mother would have ended up with one of those old downtown mansions, with orange trees in the courtyard and a view of the bay from the second floor. From her bedroom balcony, she'd have been able to glimpse boats docking at the pier, recall her pleasure trips with my father to Havana and New Orleans, before we three children were born. She'd have had her chickens in the back courtyard, and her mockingbirds, song sparrows and canaries in the open hallways. My brother Juan would've had a cattle ranch near the harbor and a sailboat in the Nautical Club. Alberto would have built a two-way highway to San Lázaro's Camino Real and the other modern hotels, like the Fénix, in the tourist zone.

And I? I would've been a pianist like all the San Lázaro girls of my era. I understood father's wish for me to become a concert pianist, bowing to the influence of tradition. Furthermore, I would have become a composer: among other pieces, I would've composed short piano pieces entitled "Short Songs to Provide Consolation" or simply "Consolation Songs." When I was twelve, I wrote three pieces in D minor, with the longest titles imaginable: "To Console Juan When He Broke His Ankle;" "To Console Dad Who Cannot See Without His Glasses;" and "To Console Mom Because She Overcooked My Birthday Cake."

I can't be sure that if my father had stayed in San Lázaro, he wouldn't have gotten a second wife, another family, another secret and intense life. And that I wouldn't have met Eduardo. For now, I must confess that months after my return from San Lázaro, my life had become a routine again, not to say normal. My children came back. Rafael and I went to welcome them home which served to bring us closer together. The house was a hubbub of joy and disorder with lots of heavy metal music. Rafael came home a drummer and that meant that his intrusive friends showed up at all hours and his syrupy girlfriends would call: "Sorry to bother you again, ma'am, but is Rafa in?"

Rafael once again was busy day in and day out at the office, in the middle of another "interesting, but difficult case." He had stopped going to Chiapas, having become fed up and disappointed by the situation. Angry at the intolerance of both parties, the many land seizures, the subterranean violence. He was angry at the Church, at the Zapatista and non-Zapatista leaders who incited the Indians to seize private lands; he was also angry at those Indians displaced from their communities for having embraced another religion and having turned against everyone. To mention Chiapas was to play with fire.

"Son, you lit the firecracker and got burnt," his mother would say to him.

"By seizing the damn lands they're not going to get justice," he'd say, stressing *damn lands*. "They're not going to get their lands back by invading them...They have to reach agreements, sit down at the table and negotiate."

When my life had resumed its usual serenity and boredom, so to speak, Rafael and I met some friends for dinner for his birthday at the San Angel Inn. Every so often

I 'd turn to the table where I had sat with Dr. Carrillo and recall the magic of that first encounter. Suddenly I saw him come into the main dining room with a woman more or less my age, perhaps a bit older. A tall attractive blonde. I blamed it all on my imagination, my whimsy, the red wine which makes my head spin: but no, it was them, following the maitre d'. When they leave, I'm sure that Eduardo will give her a box filled with little papers similar to the one he gave me: *How was it that our paths crossed?*

I pretended I hadn't seen him and began feeling really sick, but I didn't get the chance to stand up because before I knew it, Eduardo was at our table greeting us. He was polite to Rafael and our friends. He turned to me and said: "Marcela, I'd like you to meet my daughter Elizabeth. She came back from Italy just a few days ago."

"A pleasure to meet you," said Elizabeth.

"What a lovely daughter, Eduardo," I said apprehensively, shaking her hand.

I don't want to make explicit what happened after that encounter. Once, so many years ago that I don't remember when, I brought María González, the best teacher I had at the music conservatory, a short little piano piece I had composed. I gave her the scored sheet, and she patiently looked it over and then she had me play it several times.

"Play it again."

"Again?"

"Am I talking to you in Chinese?"

After playing it a few times she asked me: "Do you know what's wrong?"

"No."

"There's something superfluous," she hinted.

"Hmmm."

"Something obvious. So obvious."

"Hmmm."

"Okay, play it again."

I didn't notice it until she played the piece. I heard it

immediately, as if someone else had written it: "The ending, right?"

"If you cut all this out," she said, pointing out the notes repeating the melody. "If you finish here," she gestured like a conductor indicating when the piece is over, done with, finished, "you don't drag out the ending. You give it closure. Listen."

She played the final chord and I heard the difference.

I believe I learned my lesson; that's why the pages that follow are blank, filled with intimacy and silence.

Born in Mexico City in 1946, SILVIA MOLINA is the author of numerous novels and short story collections, including *La mañana debe seguir gris [Gray Skies Tomorrow]* which received the 1977 Xavier Villaurrutia Prize, *La familia vino del norte [The Family Came From the North]* (1987) and *Imagen de Héctor [Image of Hector]* (1990). She received the Mexican Writers Center Award in 1980, and participated in the International Writing Program at the University of Iowa in 1990. Her Story "An Orange Is an Orange", translated by Paul Pines, was published in *Pyramids of Glass: Short Fiction from Modern Mexico* (Corona Publishing, 1994).

DAVID UNGER was born in 1950 in Guatemala City. He holds a B.A. from the University of Massachusetts, Amherst, and an MFA from Columbia University. He is the U.S. coordinator of the Guadalajara International Book Fair. Among his numerous translations are *Popol Vuh*, version by Victor Montejo (Groundwood, 1999), Elena Garro's *First Love & Look for My Obituary* (Curbstone Press, 1997) and Bárbara Jacobs's *The Dead Leaves* (Curbstone Press, 1993). Publication of his own writing include *Neither Caterpillar Nor Butterfly* (poems), *The Girl in the Treehouse* (limited edition artist's book), and poems and short stories in several anthologies. He was awarded the 1998 Ivri-Nasawi Poetry Prize and the 1991 Manhattan Borough President's Award for Excellence in the Arts.

The Sor Juana Inés de la Cruz
Literature Prize

In 1993 the Guadalajara International Book Fair (FIL), the Guadalajara School of Writers (SOGEM) and the French publisher Indigo/Coté-Femmes inaugurated the Sor Juana Inés de la Cruz Prize to recognize the published work of women writers. The award was named after Sor Juana since she was the first female writer of Spanish America, and her poetry, theater and journals constitute an important contribution to the literary arts the world over.

The primary objective of the prize is to bring attention to the work of a female writer in the Spanish language; all female writers who have published a novel in the previous three years are eligible.

The prize includes publication and distribution, under a standard book contract, of the winning entry in Mexico by Fondo de Cultura Económica Press and, since 1995, translation and publication in the United States by Curbstone Press. A presentation of the award is held during the Guadalajara International Book Fair, at which time the winner is presented with a commemorative bronze sculpture of Sor Juana designed by the Portuguese sculptor Gil Simoes. The winner is a featured reader in the Los Angeles Book Festival in April, sponsored by *The Los Angeles Times*.

The winner is selected in the following manner: January, guidelines are made available to the general public; May, deadline for receiving submissions; October, decision of the judges is made public; December, award's ceremony takes place during the Guadalajara International Book Fair. Contact: SOGEM, Av. Circ. Augustín Yáñez #2839, Guadalajara, 44110, JAL, Mexico.

The prize is sponsored by Tequila Sauza S.A. de C.V.; Curbstone Press, *The Los Angeles Times*, Mayor's Office of Zapopan; The Western Technological Institute for Higher Learning, Jalisco; and General Outreach Studies, University of Guadalajara.

Other Sor Juana Inés de La Cruz Prize Winners from Curbstone Press

Assault on Paradise
a novel by Tatiana Lobo, translated by Asa Zatz
$15.95pa.   ISBN 1-880684-46-2   320pp

This fast-paced, bawdy adventure of Central America of the early 1700s vividly depicts how the Conquistadores and the Church invaded Central America, impoverishing one world to enrich another.

"On the one hand a hilarious swashbuckling adventure, on the other a bloody, bitter indictment of the Catholic Church in the colonizing of Central America, this novel deservedly won the Sor Juana Inés de la Cruz prize...The novel is kept moving rapidly by its memorable cast of characters."—*Library Journal*

"...filled with bawdy humor and wryly comic moments...*Assault on Paradise* offers a withering portrait of both the Inquisition and the Spanish conquest of the New World..."—Jay Parini, *New York Times Book Review*

First Love & Look for My Obituary
Two Novellas by Elena Garro, translated by David Unger
$11.95pa   1-880684-51-9   112pp

First Love examines the consequences of two tourists befriending German prisoners of war in France and explores the tension between primal human kindness and social conventions. *Look for My Obituary* explores a surrealistic, haunting love affair set in a world of arranged marriages.

"This small book stands out in the landscape of contemporary Mexican fiction."—Donley Watt, *Dallas Morning News*

"This talented Mexican writer transcends geographical barriers and chronology in her depiction of universal emotions and metaphysical problems."—J. Walker, *Choice*

CURBSTONE PRESS, INC.

is a non-profit publishing house dedicated to literature that reflects a commitment to social change, with an emphasis on contemporary writing from Latino, Latin American and Vietnamese cultures. Curbstone presents writers who give voice to the unheard in a language that goes beyond denunciation to celebrate, honor and teach. Curbstone builds bridges between its writers and the public – from inner-city to rural areas, colleges to community centers, children to adults. Curbstone seeks out the highest aesthetic expression of the dedication to human rights and intercultural understanding: poetry, testimonies, novels, stories, and children's books.

This mission requires ensuring that as many people as possible know about these books and read them. To achieve this, a large portion of Curbstone's schedule is dedicated to arranging tours and programs for its authors, working with public school and university teachers to enrich curricula, reaching out to underserved audiences by donating books and conducting readings and community programs, and promoting discussion in the media. It is only through these combined efforts that literature can truly make a difference.

Curbstone Press, like all non-profit presses, depends on the support of individuals, foundations, and government agencies to bring you, the reader, works of literary merit and social significance which might not find a place in commercial publishing channels, and to bring the authors and their books into communities across the country. Our sincere thanks to the many individuals who support this endeavor and to the following businesses, foundations and government agencies: Josef and Anni Albers Foundation, Connecticut Commission on the Arts, Connecticut Arts Endowment Fund, Connecticut Humanities Council, Greater Hartford Arts Council, Junior League of Hartford, Lannan Foundation, Lawson Valentine Foundation, National Endowment for the Arts, Open Society Institute, Puffin Foundation, Edward C. & Ann T. Roberts Foundation, and the U.S.-Mexico Fund for Culture.

Please support Curbstone's efforts to present the diverse voices and views that make our culture richer. Tax-deductible donations can be made by check or credit card to:
Curbstone Press, 321 Jackson Street, Willimantic, CT 06226
phone: (860) 423-5110   fax: (860) 423-9242   www.curbstone.org

IF YOU WOULD LIKE TO BE A MAJOR SPONSOR OF A
CURBSTONE BOOK, PLEASE CONTACT US.